The Franchise

Leon Clarke

ISBN 978-0-9575103-6-4

This edition © Botty Publishing Ltd 2018
Botty Publishing Ltd is a registered company founded by Richard Goodall in 2012.

"History repeats itself, first as tragedy, second as farce."
Karl Marx.

"A bad system will beat a good person every time."
W.E. Deming

1.

'Excuse me? Yes, you.' John stopped and looked at the woman. It was *his* attention she was after. Positioned behind a booth, she wore a woollen, grey suit jacket and matching knee-length skirt. The collar on her white blouse had been starched. 'You are here with the prospect of teaching abroad. That is why you are at this convention.'

Her voice was filled with enough authority to draw John closer, uncertain as to whether she had asked a question or delivered a statement.

He buttoned and unbuttoned his jacket in the three steps it took to reach the booth. His gaze roved past her to the backdrop she was half concealing. The banner was simple, a royal blue border framing a large grey building surrounded by neatly mowed grassland. On the circular desk in front of her, pamphlets were fanned out in groups of four. The same picture as that on the banner adorned the cover. 'Lyonton' was arched above it.

The woman didn't smile as he approached, nor did she lean forward or extend a hand.

'I do believe you're the right person we've been searching for.'

John wanted to ask how and why she thought that was the case. He picked up a pamphlet suspecting he had been mistaken for someone who had previously visited the stall; but then why hadn't she addressed him by a false name?

'Our facilities are practically brand new. We moved to a custom built site to accommodate all of our needs. It was the best decision for the company to bring everyone under one roof. It allows us to move forward in the direction we want to take,' she said, sounding as though she had been raised in a private school and failed to take leave of its borders. Her hair, predominantly grey, was as plastic as her legs. It was tucked in a curl and hanging above her shoulders. She reminded him of a sepia image of his grandma or a female Prime Minister, he couldn't decide. There were those who would have paid money to kneel and lick the heels of her boots.

'We are currently understaffed by approximately sixty members,' she continued, reading through the pamphlet with him. 'We estimate that next year, with the growth that has been forecast, we will bring in another one-hundred and seventy-five students to add to our burgeoning compliment. There is no pressure to increase these numbers you understand. What we want to bring to our establishment, be it students or faculty members, are the right people.'

John nodded, reluctant to stare at her face for too long. It appeared almost blurred, as if caught on camera in motion, like someone had very subtly dragged her features a fraction right of centre.

On the inside back cover of the pamphlet was the company's address, the photograph was yet again identical to the banner. The name of the city where the school was based was unfamiliar.

'Believe me, it exists. If I had a pound for every question I've received about our location, I would have retired long ago.'

John smiled, as if he appreciated the joke.

'Are there any questions you would like answering?' the woman asked, removing the pamphlet from John's hands and reinserting it back into the pack as if she was presenting a card trick. She shuffled them neatly before fanning them again. It was an art she had honed for they required no retouching. John was tempted to select another.

'You're affiliated with *the* Lyonton? The one founded in 1725? Are they expanding as a chain of schools across the globe or is it more like a franchise?' he asked, noticing that the booths adjacent and further down the corridor were filled by chatter, easy conversation, the type of discourse he had witnessed throughout the rest of the convention during the past hour. He wondered if the woman had grown bored of her scripted speech and the same repeated soundbites. She was no doubt jealous of those who had filled their vacant slots, closed up their stalls and retired to the hotel bar.

'We at Lyonton Gebjin, are educational specialists. We have a proud heritage linked to this name that we look to uphold and promote, as you can see by our crest.' The woman tapped the white emblem on the banner that sat proudly above the photograph of the building. The

Latin surrounded an image of two equine beasts standing facing each other, hooves up like boxer's gloves. The writing was disproportionately tiny; *'Cistae investigationis albo fit per scripturam'*.

'What does it mean?' John enquired.

'The horse symbolises intelligence, light and victory. The donkey symbolises foolishness and stubbornness. It's about the battle between the two and how we strive to make the horse triumphant. Is there anything else?' the woman stated, placing herself in front of the badge and motto. If he had been in charge, John wouldn't have given the animals equal footing but rather had the donkey succumbing, even if ever so slightly. He wondered how it differed, if at all, to the original Lyonton crest.

'Does the school run from nursery up to the sixth form?' he asked, conscious of the time. Another booth had just become vacant as that head teacher completed their recruitment process. Those who still had positions to fill were scheduled to be finished within the next hour. It was the second job fair John had been to in as many months and another was due to run in three weeks' time.

The first he had visited towards the end of the final term out of both curiosity and convenience. It had been held a ten-minute walk from his flat. Word had reached his current employers that he had been spotted at the event but whoever had made the remark to the upper echelons of the school had been under the false impression that he had not been forthright. He had informed the governors at the Christmas party that, as they couldn't offer him a promotion for at least two years, he would be looking elsewhere. They had at least claimed they understood. They had informed him, as a group, that he shouldn't sign anything immediately. Instead, he should return to them with his offer so they could see if there was anything they could do for him. For all his searching over the past six months, John had found nothing he believed was going to provide a quality environment to enable him to develop. Now, two weeks into the summer holidays, having returned from Rome with wanderlust, he had come to see what could be on offer in twelve months' time. Whether he was truly ready to commit to a life overseas for a couple of years, however, was an entirely different entity. Most of the stalls he had checked from afar, as though he were merely using the convention centre as a thoroughfare.

John checked over his shoulder and down at his watch, hoping someone was ready to express a real interest so he could leave.

'We specialise in everything,' the woman explained. 'From two years to eighteen. We are even looking into expanding this. I could take you through a list of all the areas we are considered to be excelling in but I assume you know what to expect from an institution of our calibre? We are certainly keen to push both Elevated Learning and Collective Collaboration.' Again, as soon as she started speaking, John averted his gaze from her face. He spent the rest of her response checking out the space surrounding her legs where there should have been boxes filled with trinkets to hand out as souvenirs to be remembered by – *if not next year, maybe the one after?* The woman shuffled her feet, her heels clicking. 'Anything else?'

There were sixty metres of corridor John had yet to traverse but he could see to the end and nothing stood out. Not that he was expecting a halo of light to shine forth from the booth of his future employer. Nothing he had heard or seen during the past couple of hours suggested that he would be ordering a new passport. Realistically, he was biding his time in the warmth so the wait on the frigid station platform wasn't too unbearable.

'I do have one more question,' John said. 'How is it possible that you know I'm the "right person you're searching for", when you don't know what it is I do?' The woman brought her hands together below her chin so her fingers became a series of X's. Her eye contact was as irregular as John's, but rather than gazing off into the space around him, her eyelids fluttered closed.

'Are you aware of how many CV's I receive every time I come to this convention? Do you know how many are genuine, one hundred percent certified? I have found that over the past two years, it is better for me to stand, observe and to watch how a person walks, conducts themselves and to look closely at what they are wearing. You do know that Sean Connery was not selected to be James Bond on the basis of his CV? Nevertheless, if you feel inclined to provide me with one, I would appreciate that,' the woman concluded, nodding at his satchel, which John found himself reaching into. He handed over a double-sided sheet. The woman accepted it without so much as checking down to discover his name. 'You're probably wondering what the next step is?' she said, withdrawing a business card from her breast pocket. 'We'll be in touch.'

2.

The following day was Saturday. John woke naturally, close to nine, and made his way to the kitchen. Having poured himself a juice and eaten two biscuits he took a shower, during which time the post was delivered. He was due to meet his parents for lunch and was contemplating the coming day as he bent to pick up the pieces of mail.

He hadn't given any real thought to his time spent at the convention centre, considering his hours there a relative waste. He'd stopped at two more stalls after Lyonton, then traipsed back to the station hungry. Failing to satisfy his stomach with a packet of crisps, he spent the duration of the journey home waiting for messages to be responded to. When asked by a colleague, who had been unable to attend the event, on whether it had been worth it, John replied that she had spent her time more wisely elsewhere. Of all the schools and the countries he mentioned from the event, Lyonton wasn't one.

He thumbed to the third and largest of the brown manila envelopes and his eyebrows furrowed. The stamp was printed in the same royal blue as the background of the Lyonton pamphlets and banner. *Lyonton*. Had it been much thicker, the postman would have been forced to ring the bell. John tore open the flap to find it filled with a multitude of documents. He pulled out the thickest and poured the rest onto the coffee table.

Dear Johnathon Downton,

Thank you and congratulations on accepting the post of Devoted Prime Educator. We have selected this post for you based on your current position and prior experience. The salary scale is on the reverse for your further consultation. Included in this package is a one-way e-ticket, a travel guide of the Gebjin area and, most importantly, the current staff handbook Edition 70 detailing expectations and standards. We look forward to greeting you in the forthcoming days for the induction process.

Kind Regards,
Margaret Gillies, Head.

John turned the page. Yet again, it was obviously a mistake. Margaret had sent it to the wrong person when posting out the applications late last night. There was no stamp or courier logo, but there had to be some rapid service put on at the behest of the convention organisers as part of their package to lure schools. Whoever it was meant for had fewer years' experience and held a far less significant position then he currently did. *Devoted Prime Educator.* It wasn't a title John had ever heard previously, but the aim of private educational establishments was to sound more pretentious to appease those paying fees.

John picked up the e-ticket to find out who the bundle was actually intended for, but yet again it had his name printed upon it. This time with his middle name, Owen, added. The flight was scheduled for Thursday at 7pm. They had allocated him two pieces of luggage and placed him in premium economy. 'Premium economy' sounded as fabricated as 'Devoted Prime Eductaor'. It reminded him of the local garage and the six tier car wash. When he had been in high school, a friend had once bragged that his dad had managed to purchase a Level 8 Super Premium Deluxe Special Car Bath Massage Plus but no one had believed him. Now it sounded less of an exaggeration.

Taking the letter headed contract to his computer, John placed his thumb underneath the number at the foot of the page. He clicked on the blue Skype icon and dialled. The tone was a long, drawn-out, droll beep. It extended for so long before reaching a pause, that John was on the brink of hanging up and concluding the whole package was a fabrication.

'Hello, Lyonton Educational Specialists. Head of Front of House Communications speaking. How may I help you?'

John could see them sporting the same austere expression Margaret had worn, staring out over their desk or whatever it was they sat at for eight hours of the day.

'Hi, is this Lyonton Gebjin?' Johnathon asked.

'We are a proud member of the Lyonton family,' the woman replied, automatically.

'Right, my name's Johnathon Downton. I've just received a package this morning through the mail.'

'Ah yes, Mr Downton, lovely to hear from you. We've been told all about you. You're one of our new Devoted Prime Educators starting next month. We have you down to arrive next Friday for our week long induction process.'

'Yes.'

'Yes. And?'

'Well, I mean you do appear to have me down to do these things but there's been a mistake,' John said. He gesticulated to the computer monitor which remained a calm blue. The call duration ticked away in large white numbers.

'And how is that?' the woman asked. She was seemingly trained to mimic Margaret's accent though it slipped occasionally. Words were spoken with a foreign inflection; *th* pronounced *s*.

'I never signed a contract. I merely handed over a copy of my CV.'

'You handed over your CV?'

'Yes. Margaret asked for it as I was leaving so I gave it to her,' John explained. He looked over at the fridge wondering if he could start on his cereal and still be heard.

'You gave it to her because you wanted the job?'

'Well, not really. I mean, I didn't get enough information. She chose me not vice versa. I walked over and listened to her and then, as I was leaving, she asked for my CV so I gave it to her.'

'Did you hand it out to everyone at the centre?'

'No.'

'But you did hand it to Margaret and you were at the fair because you were looking for a job. And now you've been given a job, but there's a mistake on our behalf?'

'Yes, there's a mistake. I've just explained that to you. I've been given a job that I haven't accepted.'

'Has this happened before?'

'What? Have I been given a job without asking for it? No, of course not. Listen, I think what has happened is that Margaret has made a mistake and mixed my CV up with someone else. Maybe there's another John or a James or Josh she saw yesterday who did sign for you,' John said, his funds for the call slipping below two pounds.

'Well, although that sounds possible, we've never encountered a mistake like this before either and, as you can imagine, we've handed out far more jobs than you have taken. So in all probability, I expect the mistake to be yours.'

John raised a threatening finger at the monitor. 'I think at this juncture you are best to put me on to Margaret personally so I can sort this out with her.'

'I'm afraid Mrs Gillies isn't on the campus.'

'I didn't expect her to be since she was still in the convention centre at five pm yesterday. However, I'm sure she has a mobile phone.'

'One second, Mr Downton.' The woman took herself literally. 'I'm afraid she's in a meeting,' she added.

'Well in that case, you can tell her to call me when she's done.'

'So you never actually signed anything?' John stared at his mum from across the circular, marble table. His dad had slipped his headphones on as soon as the meal had finished and excused himself to go and browse the hi-fi equipment. At the rate the conversation was going, John was a question away from joining him. Not that his mum's reaction was inconsistent with the retorts of those he had messaged regarding the affair. Everyone seemed to be in agreement that he had, in some way, missed out a segment of the story.

'For the nineteenth time, no.'

'I'm sorry, it just seems peculiar that's all,' his mum replied, her coffee untouched. 'Do you think they've named themselves anonymously from the real Lyonton? Just chosen a name randomly because it sounds good?'

'No, I think it is in some way affiliated with the real Lyonton, especially because the head sounded like she came from its all-girl equivalent. It's just that she was very vague when I asked what that link was,' John said, still hungry and tempted to order a second dessert since his mum was paying. She would be happy for him to do so too. He could be a stone overweight and she would still announce he looked thinner than the previous week.

'It isn't the real Lyonton, is it?'

'No Mum. As far as I'm aware Lyonton isn't an MLB franchise and hasn't upped sticks from its esteemed grounds in the borough of Lyonton, London,' John replied.

'Well, you never know with these private schools. They're run by Thatcherites to produce Thatcherites. Bottom line, market forces; there will be cheaper rent and higher paying fees out there, and let's face it, it's a backdoor into preserving some sort of colonial base,' she said, finally picking up her cup. 'And the head hasn't called you back?'

John took out his phone.

'If she hasn't done so by the time I'm home, I'll call again. To be honest, the image I have is a market stall filled with fake Adidas and Nike bags. From afar you think you're heading for a bargain but then up close you can see the stitching about to come loose, the brand name is peeling off and you need a set of safety pins after the zip disintegrates in your hand.'

'I think you're being overly pessimistic,' his mum replied, calling the waiter across, apparently still peckish. 'I think it shows ambition. Look at Jose Saramago using **The Double** as a title. The man's a Nobel Prize winner not some cheap knock-off Dostoyevsky. How about The Verve? Are they some faux ELP because they named a song *Lucky Man*? What...'

'It's okay, Mum, I understand. It's a long way from the original point I made but I understand.'

'Well that's good then, darling. What? Are you not staying for your sticky toffee pudding?' she asked, as he stood, swiping his jacket from the back of his chair.

'No, I'm good. Dad will probably eat it. I'm going for a walk. Thanks for lunch. I'll give you a call tomorrow.'

The sky was overcast and a drizzle fell. It was light enough, however, that John wasn't conscious of it at first despite hordes of people with umbrellas hoisted above their heads. It struck him to ask someone at random what they thought of his situation. If they could see how far-fetched it sounded. If they could take his side rather than suspect he was at fault for the misunderstanding. However there were enough people clamouring for their attention on the pedestrian paths already, jumping out with clipboards at hand.

One of them caught John unaware, bouncing up to him. His colourful mac flapped in a way that suggested he was going to present something else entirely. Were these the people who had become accustomed to rejection at high school or were they the ones who never went home alone on a Friday night? John swatted the man away before he could unleash his prescribed spiel. He carried straight up the street. A second person, this time jangling a bucket, darted out at him as though he had requested a large scale game of whack-a-mole.

'No,' John said firmly, ducking out of the rain and underneath the awning of a mall. The door was almost pushed into him. He dodged it, and the woman busy with her umbrella, slipped inside and headed up the escalator.

The cinema's list of features and their times flashed up on a board. A couple of showings that piqued John's interest were due to start shortly but he found himself indecisive; the thought of the contract and the plane ticket on his coffee table were too much of a distraction. The receptionist who had taken his call had obviously forgotten to relay his message and so he moved along to a quiet seat in a café and brought out his phone again.

'Hello, Lyonton Educational Specialists. Head of Front of House Incoming Communications speaking. How may I help?'

'Hi, it's Johnathon Downton. I called about,' he checked his watch, 'three hours ago. I asked you to inform Margaret Gillies she was to call me once she was out of her meeting.'

'I'm sorry, sir, I wasn't here three hours ago. I've only been at the desk for twenty minutes,' the woman explained, her voice identical to the last receptionist. Still, as excuses went.

'In that case, so as to not make any false accusations if I have to call again, could I ask your name?'

'Certainly, my name's Ann. I'm the Head Front of House for Incoming Communications,' she replied cheerfully.

John was about to ask if that wasn't her colleague's title but felt it was in his interest to remain pertinent.

'Ann, is it possible to speak to Margaret Gillies now?' he asked, watching the baristas shuffle back and forth.

'I'm afraid Mrs Gillies is in a meeting now,' Ann replied, as someone else spoke to her. 'Please hold for one second,' she added, covering the mouthpiece, allowing John to retract the phone to see how much credit remained. When he returned it to his ear, he could hear the muffled sound of conversation in a foreign language. Ann might as well have removed her palm and yelled down the line.

Beside John, someone enquired if the chair next to him was occupied then, without pausing for breath, asked if they could take it. John shook his head then nodded.

'Hello Mr Downton, I'm sorry about that. I've just been informed that Margaret is not expected back in Lyonton for the forthcoming week as she is conducting interviews and then taking personal leave. Can I take a message for her?'

'I thought that she was in a meeting earlier?' John replied, glancing up to find the man with desires over the chair still loitering as though in the midst of a freeze frame. Once eye contact was made he shook his head, then nodded.

'She certainly was in a meeting earlier today. She has an intensive schedule.'

'One so intensive she doesn't have time to make a call to her alleged new hire?' John replied, nodding at the man, whose hands, having reached the top of the chair, suddenly retracted.

'Is it taken?' he mouthed.

'Extremely intensive,' the receptionist remarked. 'Although according to her official timetable, there isn't anything down about calling you,' she added, the person she had been conversing with still idling beside her. John shook his head and the man's hands went back to the chair.

'So can I take it?'

'What about if I slot it into her schedule for a week today?'

'A week today? No, it will be too late by then. I'm due to leave on Thursday. How about her deputy or assistant? Can I talk to one of them?' There was a pause. John could hear the receptionist and her colleague shaking their heads.

'I am afraid we are in the middle of a recruitment process at present. If Mrs Gillies is the person you must speak to, you really should wait until she becomes available. I can book you a slot?'

'Like the previous receptionist? You know what, it doesn't matter. Forget about it,' John said, gesticulating to the man that he was undoubtedly welcome to take the chair.

'Well, there's no need to be like that.'
'That's good. Is there anything else I can do for you?'

4.

John found that over the next few days he had a serious case of the Baader-Meinhofs. Everything made allusions to a city he hadn't previously known existed. Had the question of Gebjin's coordinates been raised prior to Friday's meeting with Margaret, he would have been tempted to state it was located within the realms of a Tolkien of Pratchett novel. Yet here it was on the side bar of the TV; it was on the Wikipedia Page of the Day. In the free magazine he grabbed on the bus to act as an impromptu umbrella, there was an article on global franchises that captured enough of his attention to leave him soggy.

Therefore, with all roads appearing to lead to this new destination, on Wednesday afternoon, John took the handbook from the coffee table and gave it a thorough read. As handbooks went it was as generic as any other. A pro forma downloaded from the internet with the Lyonton crest inserted at the top as though that were enough to stave off allegations of plagiarism.

The package on offer was good, even when taking into account his place a rung lower on the salary scale than his experience dictated. If it was simply a case of numeration there was no argument. The monthly salary was also complimented by an annual bonus. There was a gym, tennis courts and a swimming pool on site. Free accommodation was provided in a two-bedroom flat behind the main school building. They would pay for his flight home at the end of the two-year contract unless he felt so inclined to stay. If only it was known by any other name.

It had John recalling a holiday when he went searching for a birthday present for his mum. One store had been recommended for its leather craftsmanship and indeed the quality was exceptionally high. Yet rather than being satisfied with creating their own satchels and handbags and charging a reasonable rate, the proprietors had added symbols and badges. Then they had embossed the leather with *Made in Paris* or *Made in Milan*, leaving the finished product crass, spoilt and undeniably fake.

All the same John thought, after turning off the bedroom light, this wasn't a backyard enterprise that could be shut down and relocated at a yelped code word. This was an institution flaunting a name and symbol that had a three hundred year legacy to uphold. The link between them had to be strong.

It was his mum who woke him from dreams of spreadsheets, bank accounts and serious men parading halls in black gowns with stern faces, scrolls in hand. There were blue skies and sunny afternoons. A tennis racket in one hand, a sour lemonade in the other and a female trainer in a pleated skirt laughing at his quips. His mum had let herself in and was examining the lounge as though he still had that week's pocket money to earn.

'I've brought you one of our larger suitcases for packing,' she announced, as he poked his head around the corner. 'Cup of tea? Bacon butty?' she added, removing the milk from the fridge, the kettle already on. 'Dad asked if you'll be wanting a lift to the airport? The queues were shocking last time. There were passengers lined up on the main road and the airport staff were standing around like it was acceptable. Does that not present more of a threat? Where have you moved your sugar?'

'It's where it always resides unless you place it somewhere else. Top cupboard,' John said, pulling on a pair of jeans. 'So, you think I should definitely go?' he asked, as he emerged into the kitchen.

'Well that's entirely up to you darling. You hadn't said anything about it for the past couple of days so we assumed the answer was still yes.'

'I thought from what I had said over the weekend my answer was most likely no,' he replied, collating all the documentation back into a neat pile on the coffee table. His mum shrugged.

'Well if that's the case keep the suitcase for your next holiday. It took your dad half an hour to bring it down from the loft. You know how much of an ordeal that is,' she said, placing the sugar into the equivalent drawer as to the one she would at home. 'Do you want me to make a packing list?' she added, reaching for the neatly stacked paraphernalia. Again her comments revolved around the clean-cut building set solid amidst the lush green grass.

'I think I should be alright. I was just about to go out for a jog,' John said, stretching, able to touch the ceiling.

'In your jeans?' his mum replied, settling down into the armchair. 'Don't worry, if I need to go before you've returned, I'll see myself out. Make sure you put a jumper on as well. It's chilly out.'

John dodged the puddles and sludge as he ran down the stony path that led through the woods. A couple of dogs yapped and pulled on their leads as he burst past. Flecks of mud splattered the bare skin of his legs.

Aside from a couple of variations that lengthened or shortened the route, it was the same one John had been jogging his entire life and all of a sudden he felt numbed by the sense of mundanity. He had experienced similar feelings to this before. Jogging did after all allow time to contemplate all there was in life. It was true that, on occasion, his legs had been forced to carry the rest of his body around the three and a half miles against their wish. There were times when his brain had begged the question, "What if we stop, walk and go and do something else instead?" But this time it was different. He felt beyond apathetic. He was nullified by sight of the trees, the leaves and the scraggy nettles lurking from beneath the cracks in the dry wall. The prospect of demanding one final push up the hill was dispiriting. His enthusiasm waned for the process of starting and finishing at the front door, whether it was his or his parents' five streets away. It would be the same in two days', two weeks, two months. He would be grey. His skin would be set full of wrinkles and the path wouldn't have changed. He could have emerged onto the main road early or, for the sake of a totally new tangent, lost himself in a high rise estate, but where was the exhilaration in that? Why else had he visited two conferences if not to expand his horizons further than a detour during a light jog? Every part of him was pleading for something new. A jump into the ocean or a blind date of extreme proportions. So why wasn't he being pulled by magnetic force to the adventure waiting beyond the airport?

He ambled past a crumbling brick wall and a set of railings bald of their chipped paint, their thin bodies wearing crisp packets as though it were a makeshift abacus. It was downhill to the petrol station, then it plateaued to the mechanic's.

Two years. Twenty-four months. It wasn't even that when you subtracted the holidays. And if it wasn't his ticket like he'd tried to tell them? That was okay, the suitcase could be used for a holiday.

5.

The plane was eerily still. From John's position slightly to the right of centre, row 34D, neither the front nor the back of the aircraft was visible. It hadn't appeared to extend to such an extent from the terminal gate, but once inside it had taken on the dimensions of the Tardis. The steps into the upper deck rose so high there may have been additional levels rather than just one. There was a feeling that they were moving on a travellator within the realms of a hotel.

Whilst sitting at the gate, John had made attempts to predict those who were also bound for Lyonton, however, with such a vast array of people, he soon gave up. Now though, headphones in and halfway through the flight, he began checking again. The majority of those around him were sleeping. A couple of people were stretching their legs in the darkness, lit only intermittently by flickering screens and the rays of the overhead reading lights. There was a woman in her late thirties carrying a baby back and forth. She passed it from arm to arm, its murmurs of discontent rising only when the mother paused to turn. A couple of rows in front, a father had a young child hanging off each leg, whilst the third and eldest hauled herself up his back.

'Excuse me, sir, would you care for anything else to drink?' a steward suddenly asked.

'An orange juice?' John replied, receiving a nod that suggested he had made an enlightened decision. John wondered whether the airline only employed people from certain counties or if elocution lessons came as part of the training. He rubbed underneath his eyes and resumed his search for colleagues. Though what was it he was expecting to spot? Single people in their late twenties to thirties sporting looks of confusion and subtly analysing the other passengers? After all, Margaret had said he was what they were looking for. Even if his employment was technically a case of mistaken identity, that didn't alter what she had claimed. Yet as far as he could see, his doppelganger was not aboard.

John pointed his toes to stretch his calves, giving up on his attempt to find kindred co-workers. Since he had received the documentation he had been certain his plight was uncommon, a case of one in millions. Yet by the way his parents and everyone else had reacted, perhaps this occurred with a greater frequency. Paperwork was passed from one person to another, deadlines had to be met, a card was dropped, picked up and slotted into the wrong place. In a large scale organisation there had to be mistakes of this magnitude being made, if not with regularity, then at least with some recurrence.

The steward came and leaned across, handing him not just a juice but also a couple of mini chocolate chip cookies.

'They're on the house,' he said, with a knowing nod. John responded with one of his own, eating a cookie as he watched the steward strut down the aisle, hips sashaying in an identical manner as his female workfellows.

John downed the juice. He was about to pop the second cookie in his mouth when a girl of six or seven stopped by his chair, hands upon her hips.

'Where did you get that?' she asked, barefoot, dressed in a football shirt that acted as a nightie. It was one that didn't belong to any team John recognised.

'Where did you get that shirt from?'

'My daddy bought it. He has one as well. And my mummy. And my sisters. Now, what about your cookie?'

'The steward gave me it when he came over with my orange juice,' John said, the chocolate beginning to melt on the edge of his thumb and forefinger.

'Do you think that there will be any left?' the girl asked, a finger winding through the ringlets of her chestnut hair.

'I imagine so. I wouldn't expect I'd been given the final two with half the journey to go. I'm not that important.'

'But what if that is the case?' the girl queried, gaze not wavering.

'Well, I wasn't aware they were available until I received them and you weren't until you saw me, so I doubt its widespread knowledge. However, they might be rolling around in them or using them to play draughts in business class, first class, super club class or whatever it's called rising way above us on those upper decks.'

'Can't you just give me the cookie?'

'It's started to melt.'

'That's alright,' the girl replied, daintily plucking it from his fingers, ready to spin in the fashion of a ballerina and leap down the aisle to freedom, when John asked her to wait. She did as requested in a mock statue pose with one leg off the ground, though the cookie she swallowed whole.

'You don't by any chance go to Lyonton do you?'

The girl's look of inquisitiveness morphed into a glare. She scanned those in their immediate vicinity and with the remnants of the cookie hiding many of her teeth, leaned over to inform him; 'Mummy and Daddy say we're not allowed to use that word anymore.' As to why, she didn't say. She skipped off into the darkness without looking back, leaving John's query to hang heavy until he decided to answer it himself.

'Must have misheard me,' he muttered.

6.

It was at the baggage carousel where John finally came face to face with new colleagues, though this was not apparent to them. He appeared to be the only one who had arrived without plastering Lyonton stickers, complete with the campus address, across every piece of luggage.

First he spotted a man of South Asian descent, squat with a haircut administered by the Marines. His smile was a permanent feature, as though hauling bags off the belt delighted him. Which if indeed were true made sense, because he was surrounded by six and still wasn't done.

Next was a woman in her mid-twenties who believed 1970's East Germany had been the apex of the fashion. Engaged in conversation with her was a gentleman ready for the beach. His body tapered down to a pair of battered leather sandals. He was seemingly unconcerned by his four year-old running out from between his legs to vault on and off the carousel.

The others that were to join John at Lyonton were each as different in creed, height, weight and allure, leaving John to believe that if it were his "look" he had been selected for, it was to slot in as a member of a life-size *Guess Who?*

Without so much as registering eye contact with any of them, he slung his bag onto his back and wheeled the other out through customs. He was followed as he went by uniformed officials and obedient dogs. One recent arrival was hanging his head shamefully beside an inspection table as an apple was pointed at and a piece of paper was pushed into his face. A dog routed through the man's clothes, searching for a second prize and suddenly conscious of the chocolate his mum had insisted on packing, John hurried in the most relaxed fashion possible to the exit.

In the arrival hall, holding a sign bearing the Lyonton emblem, were a couple who bore the hallmarks of friendly, caring grandparents. They were slightly grey, smiling, offering out their hands, of an almost equal height and stature. The lady stated that she was happy to take care of his bags, whilst the man removed his wallet to offer him a loan for a Starbucks coffee. John, however, waved the gesture away having been handed a week's worth of notes by his mum.

The façade and inner furnishings of the Starbucks was indistinguishable to every other one John had ever seen. Indeed, the majority of drinks on offer were identical to those in the airport he had just flown from. However, on the brink of ordering a slice of cheesecake to compliment his drink, he stopped short when he realised the spotted filling was not chocolate or fruit, but rather a fish paste. Recoiling in horror, he narrowly avoided contact with a local man who, as though he was going to be beaten to them, yelled his order for the remaining two slices. John paid, calculating the price at a fifteen percent reduction to home.

Having been shown aboard one of four eighteen-seater minibuses, all of which proudly sported his new employer's emblem on the rear, John closed his eyes. He consulted with himself as to whether, in a blind taste test, he would be able to distinguish between the mocha he was now drinking and the one he had supped eleven hours ago. After two sips he declared it would be the case.

A new colleague, who had taken the seat beside him and was wearing a sheep-herder's flat cap, enquired if he was feeling under the weather. John insisted that he was fine. He thought about asking if the man had packed his border collie but instead explained what he had been doing.

'I suppose that although there's an attempt to recreate the familiarity of the brand and your experience inside its walls regardless of your location on the globe (which indeed is the point, because your purchase of the product is based on the name and is backed up with your prior experiences and knowledge of its quality) there has to be marked differences in the end product from the original in Seattle.

'The visible merchandise will be the simplest to recreate and is probably shipped from one or two super-warehouses. The actual coffee, however, can't be made with the same water. The beans will be different. The milk and the staff are another thing entirely.'

John nodded.

'You know, I've always wondered, there's obviously a formal code of conduct and training, but who would oversee all that?' he asked, the bobbing head transferred to his colleague. 'And although there must be overseers from the top down, by the bottom rung of the pyramid, when you're actually inside singular outlets, the actions of the individual have to be as significant as the company's mission statement. I mean who is ultimately responsible for this very branch here?' John queried, as they passed another doing its regular trade. 'Is there someone at the original Starbucks HQ who is aware of this in a physical sense? A person who has actually been inside it? Witnessed its service? Can ultimately close it because they are bringing the brand into disrepute?'

'A nameless, faceless group of men,' his new colleague replied, making a formal introduction, which included outlining his post. It had double the amount of words in the title than John's own. John explained his job description, dropping both Devoted and Primary.

For the remaining half-hour journey, they discussed past positions and discovered a common appreciation for racquet sports. It was reassuring to find someone who shared vested interests and both assured the other that, once they were settled, they would find time on a court.

Such a pact was made as they arrived at the picturesque grounds that had adorned both the banner and pamphlets; the image central to luring those aboard the buses across two continents. What had been cropped from the promotional picture was the imposing outer entrance. Manning the sets of gates was a team of guards in black uniforms, all of whom appeared to be skipping school for a day's paid work. They saluted the buses as the retractable fence rolled back, allowing the newly recruited to view the grounds exactly how they appeared in the photograph, albeit with an added team of local groundskeepers. The gardeners, with bin liners in one hand and implements in the other, gave the merest of glances before casting their heads back down low to the earth. John wasn't certain, having just caught a glimpse, but it looked like they were cutting the grass with scissors usually reserved for primary classrooms.

The buses parked at the rear of the school building where a subsidiary block of flats stood. They resembled a Scottish tenement, hastily built with cheap, coarse materials. There were various stains decorating the façade of the four storeys, large swathes of plaster smeared in ugly patches attempting to cover them. It was here where everyone lived for the first twelve months, with the option to move to off-site available midway through their contract.

To welcome them were three well-dressed local women, two of whom were standing and smiling, effused with excitement at the sight of the new staff. One was strikingly attractive; tall, slender, with a bleached complexion. The other, with her hair in a blunt bob, was short and dumpy. She was holding the clipboard and papers, nodding respectfully to each face that passed.

She was not the person in overall charge, however, for behind them lay a stately woman slouched in a reclining chair positioned way back in the safety of the shade. She was dressed ready for a funeral, beadily eyeing those who stepped from the buses, her lips sucked tight. Gently she waved a lace fan, the action appearing to drain any remnants of energy she possessed.

'So welcome, welcome. I am Kaley. Please if you all look behind you this building is separated into four blocks,' the dumpy woman announced enthusiastically. 'When I call your name please come and take your set of keys. Tonight dinner will be served in the canteen at six. If you have any questions before then, please find me in the main reception,' she added, though ten hands had already been raised within the group. John watched everyone gradually disperse, his the penultimate name to be called.

'See you in a couple of hours,' the attractive woman said, with enough delicacy that John turned after a few steps to check whether her gaze had followed him. Alas, by the time he did, she and Kaley were walking past their boss, who gave them the subtlest of acknowledgements. She raised a leather handled cat 'o' nine tails that had been concealed in her lap, dropping the strips of leather softly into her open palm. Following her understudies, she nodded in time with the gentle flicking of her wrist.

John's flat was on the ground floor to the left of the lift. The walls had once been white. On the kitchen table were two bags mainly filled with basic IKEA utensils. He rooted through them to ascertain if there was anything interesting, discovering a set of meat cleavers that would have left a butcher envious.

Beside the bags were a couple of laminated cards explaining the process of electricity readings and his gas card.

You cannot top up your gas card unless the level has dropped below 30 credits. However, if your credits fall below 35, you will be fined a 10 charge credit when you go to top up.

John read it a third time to make sure it was the sentence and not himself, located the gas box to find his credit level was 185.34 and dismissed it as a typo.

The two bedrooms were of a similar size, whilst at the end of his corridor the bathroom had been put together in the five minutes the labourers had left before their contracts expired. A spirit level hadn't been used and the tiles had been thrown against the cement. If there had been a greater extent of Polyfilla, John would have suspected they owned shares in the mixing plant.

At precisely six 'o' clock, so as not to be the first to arrive, John locked his room and sauntered to the canteen having already delegated new homes to all the items from his two suitcases. He was surprised to find a group of around fifteen heading out of the main building, led by the Kaley. In the middle of the group was Ron, who welcomed him in as they met at the door and began to make introductions to some of the others who had been taken on a tour.

'Tour?' John enquired, collecting a tray and cutlery, the hot plates manned behind a long section of glass by women in white overalls.

'What they're serving isn't radioactive is it?' quipped a woman, as each of the orderlies scooped a little from her section and dumped it into a large bowl.

'A few of us had gone out into that communal area and Kaley asked if we wanted to be shown round. I would have come and knocked if I'd known your room.'

John insisted there were no hard feelings.

'So what's it like?' he asked. 'Nice set of badminton courts?'

'There's a squash court too,' smirked Carl, who shared a resemblance to Jude Law and the same job title as John.

'Really?'

'Well, no,' Ron began. 'It was supposed to be a squash court but they stuck a pillar in the centre of it.'

'They did what? How? Wasn't there a plan? A blueprint to follow?'

'Kaley couldn't explain, could she.'

Carl shook his head, his fork wagging above his plate.

'There's also an Olympic sized pool,' he said, eyebrows raised, leaving Ron to complete the explanation.

'With seven lanes.'

'Seven, not eight? Olympic pools still have eight lanes, right?' John asked, pushing his dessert around with the tail end of his spoon, expecting it to strike back, the outer texture alarmingly similar to the fish-paste cheesecake.

'Actually an Olympic pool has ten lanes. The two on the outside are never used because the water is displaced outwardly by the competitors and rebounds against the side of the pool to create turbulence. It's therefore to your benefit to be in the middle lanes so as to be least impacted by the force,' Carl explained, remarking, as an afterthought, that although the meal was filling it could have been exemplary if he could have washed it down with a beer.

8.

Having spent the majority of the night in a semi-permanent sleep, John sat yawning beside his fruit basket as he analysed the week's schedule. His jeans and shirt were fresh but in need of an iron. The fruit had already started to turn. He took a sip from his bottled water and headed in the direction of what he believed to be the Theatre Hall.

Entering the main building he found himself caught in a stream of people, faces both familiar and not, heading west at a mild, audible shuffle. John joined without uttering a syllable. He watched as old hands reunited with handshakes without pausing. Those who had been there before led the procession into a cavernous grey hall, half filled with rows of tightly packed chairs facing a black stage, either side of which were dark curtains blocking off any natural light. The stage was empty aside for a lectern with the Lyonton emblem embossed in the middle. The ceiling was a mass of worming ribbed pipes mindlessly whirring away. Air conditioning was coming from somewhere. John found a seat near the middle, second row from the back.

'Hello,' he said, offering his hand to the man he'd sat beside.

'Serge,' the man replied, 'pleasure to make your acquaintance,' he added, his cockney accent indistinct. 'How was yesterday?' he added, facing the stage, as if were he to look away he would miss something of great importance.

John shrugged: 'Everything was okay, I guess. How long have you been here for?'

'Just a year,' Serge replied, his hands oversized, the fingers sausage rolls. He bit at the skin around the nail of his index, the layer underneath was pink and raw. John watched the second hand on the wall-clock tick. People continued to wander into the room in singles and pairs, a mixture of locals and foreigners. The split was about fifty-fifty, the seating set-up close to an apartheid. A rustling from behind the curtain, stage left, reduced the decibel level to a reticent hush.

'Here comes the Gaffa,' Serge said, his smirk similar to the one pulled by Carl at dinner the previous evening. John focussed, like everyone else now, on the quivering curtain, but the person who emerged from it was not Margaret. It was a hulking mass of man clipped tightly by a suit fighting to contain him. He stopped at the lectern, belittling it, hands resting either side of the microphone, a child's toy in comparison to his frame. His head moved like an owl's, surveying the landscape. The turkey skin of his neck was pinched by the top button of his shirt. He licked his lips. His scarlet tie fell beneath the start of his zipper.

'Sorry, but who is he?' John whispered.

'The Gaffa. The Head Honcho. The Big Cheese.' Serge said, withdrawing his hands from the clasp they'd been in, as if the girth needed to be specified.

'But I thought Margaret was the head?'

'Margaret? Margaret Gillies? No, no, whatever made you think that?'

'The fact that that's what she called herself when I met her at the job fair,' John said. The droning emitting from the pipes overhead abruptly stopped so the head could clearly be heard.

'Each new year spawns the dawn of a new era here at Lyonton. I am delighted to see before me so many fresh faces ready to take on the challenge with those of us who have been building upon our prior successes. I am certain that every single one of us is keen to make sure that we hit the ground running so we are able to deliver on the promises that we made to everyone involved within the organisation at the culmination of last year.'

'Yeah,' Serge whispered, leaning forward. 'You have to be careful of that around here. She is our Head of Staff Recruitment, Renewal and Replenishment, but like with a lot of people who work at Lyonton Gebjin, they find it easier to shorten it to "Head". Don't worry,' - he noted John's glimpse of confusion - 'You'll quickly come to understand the linguistics and workings of the joint.'

He concluded as the screens either side of the stage were lit up by a PowerPoint and the head duly began to address the individual points that had been raised and dealt with over the summer as though he was running for re-election.

Scanning the room, John sensed that although the attention of the crowd was apparently focussed on the speech, their minds were elsewhere.

'...therefore we are still presently collating the results of the questionnaires that you completed and, as such, we are not prepared to rush into any of the matters before we feel a satisfactory amount of time has been spent decoding such results...'

A couple of people had started casting glances at their watches. John's gaze strayed to the side walls to mottoes that hung from giant banners. Half an ear was good enough to follow the current ICT budget and the expenditure projections for the forthcoming two years.

Committed to Desire.
Willing to Succeed.
Determined to Develop.
Promise to Perform.

Underneath each, in gold italics, was the same slogan, *Lead Not Dread*.

'Err...'

'Don't go worrying yourself about it,' Serge said, dismissing the question with a wave of the hand. 'Look, from the size and shape of you, what you *do* need to know is that we've a five 'a' side team who go for a kick about on a Friday afternoon on the pitch.'

'Sounds good,' John replied, formulating alternative slogans in his mind – *Gold Not Glitter*. 'And what is it you do?' he asked.

'I'm Head. Of Exemplary Post-Primary Sports and Physical Exercise and Recreation Pursuits. Secondary isn't a term that's used as they don't want anyone attributing negative connotations with it.'

'So, you're Head of Secondary PE?'

'Well, not exactly. As the title suggests.'

Just how much irony the statement came with, John was unsure.

'So, I haven't borne witness myself, yet,' John said, 'but I was told that the squash court has a pillar in the middle of it and the "International" pool is only seven lanes wide.'

Serge raised his hands to protest his innocence and John noted that a couple of fingers on each were squared off, as though they'd been sanded down.

'Happened before my time that. You want a history on them, best ask our HOAASTSD about the reasons. When you do, you can query why there's no running track around the pitches too. You can't miss him. He's bald with a goatee and wears a pair of shorts even when it's minus ten. In the meantime, don't forget to bring your boots on Friday,' he concluded, as the PowerPoint came to an end.

'All that is left for me to say at this juncture then,' the head announced, beads of sweat forming by his temples, 'is that I wish you all the best and look forward to seeing you at your desks providing our clientele with the best possible service.'

9.

Despite the rising number of questions competing to be answered, John didn't loiter in the hope of speaking to someone. Instead he filed out with the rest of his colleagues who had begun dissecting the speech. Lunch was already being served and after it they were to meet in their teams where John expected a full briefing would be delivered. He found Carl and Ron, the latter in a new hat, a straw boater with a bold blue band.

'Have you heard?' Ron asked, as John sat, his plate filled only with those foods he trusted from yesterday.

'Heard what?'

'You know the tall girl that greeted us yesterday?'

'The attractive one?'

'That will be her. Left. No longer employed here.'

'What? How? Why?' John blurted, his attempt to sound untroubled by such news a failure.

'Ursula,' Carl said, the reference requiring no explanation. 'Not happy with the way she works apparently.'

'According to whom?' John asked, feeling like there was a loop he was already outside of.

'According to people,' Ron added, his gaze not falling on anyone in particular.

John wanted to ask if there was a handshake he ought to be introduced to or a saying he hadn't yet had the privilege of being passed.

Having finished their lunch, they stacked away their trays and John walked with Carl to the room that had been delegated for their primary staff briefing. Carl was keen to know why he had accepted the position and John informed him it had been on a whim, a snap decision that felt like it had been made for him. When he posed the identical question to Carl, whom at 6'1" was taller than John had previously thought, the response was half mumbled. It was a divorce; the ability to spend time away to reflect. John therefore broached the safer subject of football and explained he'd heard there was five-a-side to be played.

In the midst of discussing players and making comparisons to their own games, they came upon a room filled with people who had crowded around the few desks that had been placed in no discernible pattern. Those who were not new to the establishment had laptops out in their confined spaces and were conversing in whispers with those beside them.

With no further seating available, John and Carl reclined against the wall and proceeded to wait. They weren't the last to arrive and those who entered well past the scheduled starting time filed in alongside next to them. A few presented hands and names, a couple offered warm greetings to friends they hadn't seen for the past two months. The final person to enter was hidden behind a stack of boxes. She peered out from the side of them, doing well to hide any signs of the strain being placed upon her. John felt etiquette demanded he go and offer help. However, he was on the far side of the room, wedged on the wrong side of a desk and no one else made any movement towards her so he merely swayed on his heels.

'Hello, excuse me, sorry Mrs Welk, Mr Shaft, Miss Pond, Mr Craft and Mr Latte say they won't be able to make the meeting. Apologies from them,' the woman said sheepishly, her white blouse on the verge of being ripped from her shoulders by the weight of the load she was balancing.

'What? Not one of them? They didn't think to email this out?' said a woman, slamming the lid of her laptop closed.

'They are all too busy.'

'Doing what?' the woman demanded, as the others on their laptops rolled their eyes.

'They are all in a meeting.'

'But this is a meeting. This is a very important meeting. How can they schedule something simultaneously? I'm sorry Kate, it's not your fault,' the woman said, calming quickly, her sigh drawn out. Kate, an anglicised name the secretary had selected after her favourite actress, apologised again: 'I believe their meeting was about this one but it has overrun.'

'Typical,' the woman said, sitting back and folding her arms, her lips reverberating as she exhaled, leaving Kate to attempt a curtsy as she exited.

Those who had already spent a year or more at the establishment walked out, whilst those new to such news held their ground assuming there would be further clarification and direction. As she reached the door, the woman who had put forth the questions to Kate paused, sensing that any explanation was now hers to deliver.

'Sorry, my name's Jenny,' she said. 'I guess if you want to come with me I can offer some broad clarification as to what to expect over the forthcoming days, weeks and months,' she added. 'It would make more sense if we exited the campus though,' she continued, trudging down the corridor, followed by a group of eight, who stuck closely together.

Rather than leaving past the security guards at the front, Jenny led them right, through the resident's block and along the back wall to a corrugated iron door.

'You'll really want to go and ask The Facilities and Maintenance of Internal Campus Operations for one of these keys. I'd tell you where to find them, but they move home quicker than Elizabeth Taylor,' she said, as they found themselves on an awkwardly shaped cobbled courtyard which was home to three decrepit scooters and a wave of litter that had been swept to the sides. 'Down that way,' Jenny continued, pointing at the alley straight ahead, 'there's a couple of useful shops: stationary, snacks, that sort of thing. To the right there's a first-rate restaurant. It's not marked by any signs but if the lights on behind the sliding glass door, it's open. You can take your own booze,' she said, turning left. 'We're going to wander round to the front of the building,' she added. The path was mainly adobe, though broken bricks and other materials lined the floor of the narrow ginnel.

'Allow me to give you all a quick history. The school, or at least the brand name, has been going strong in Gebjin for six years. Last year we moved to this purpose-built site instead of being on three separate campuses. With it, as you will know, came the new philosophy in education that we are pioneering.'

'Sorry,' John asked, third in line, 'what do you mean "new philosophy", you mean Elevated Learning and Collective Collaboration.'

'It's not really "new" per se is it,' Carl added from the back.

Jenny halted and turned to gauge how many were in the dark.

'You mean you don't know?' she asked. Three-quarters of the group shook their heads. 'So you've come here…okay, well, basically, you all know that schools are always chasing their tails in education wanting to be at the forefront of learning? Well one of the board members of the Lyonton "family" received a government Trace Paper. The developments here are to put us, not just one, but several steps ahead of the competition in the city and across the globe. The crux of the paper's findings was that teachers distract from children's learning.

Their presence in the room provides discussion and takes vital time away from the children staring at paper doing calculations and practising their handwriting. What was also pointed out was that from a safeguarding perspective, it was far better not to risk having anyone over eighteen interacting or having any direct contact with the children.'

'Sorry? No direct contact? Does this mean we're required?'

'Oh, but we are required. If we weren't here to set up appropriate levelled tasks, who knows what they might do,' Jenny said, now walking backwards, navigating the alleys with short glances over her shoulder.

'But if we can't have any contact with them, how do we deliver these tasks?' John asked, from behind a small, smartly dressed ginger-haired girl, the group now squeezed down into single file.

'You enter them into a server which filters the sheets for any inappropriate content and then distributes them to the children, most of whom receive their work at home. To them it looks as though a computer has randomly selected what they are to do for the day.'

'And what about the minority who don't access their work from home?' Carl enquired, the main road coming into view.

'The school have set up what they call "soft pockets" because they're completely padded on the inside. Lyonton's aim is to have everyone using these within the next five years since they charge the pupils attending them an annual residence fee. They are monitored by CCTV, except they're not, because nobody wants to be accused of spying and, God forbid, some pervert manages to gain access into the control room.' Jenny paused and sighed.

'I can see the doubt on some of your faces but you'll soon come to discover what an excellent system it is and realise how advanced we are. Honestly we're so far ahead of the curve even the Scandinavians aren't doing it yet.'

10.

With the following day being the final inset and with no further instruction as how to spend the remainder of this one, John decided to be proactive and sort out his workspace. In his previous jobs he would have been directed to it in order to give him time to prepare it accordingly. The extra hours of independence would also give him the chance to research the institution and the methodology he had just been informed about. He was certain he would have noticed this major development in teaching and learning when he had checked on the school's website or in the package they had sent in the post.

As he strode down the corridors, their imposing size hardened by a lack of decoration, the few people he passed walked without acknowledgement. They were focussing on phones, busy, or at least wanting to appear so, leaving John to traverse the passages and locate the Educational Curriculum Transfer Hall through trial and error.

The main workspace was cavernous, a grand room that dwarfed the theatre. It was built high and spiralled towards a conical apex. The ground floor was packed tight with strict rows of desks, each cordoned off into its own cubicle by a five-foot-high matte silver privacy screen. On each of the four storeys above ran wrought iron mezzanines overlooking the hundred or so cubicles. How these upper decks were reached, however, John was unsure. As far as he could see there were no internal staircases or ladders.

The walls of the hall were a similar dull grey to the cubicle screens, though the majority of them had been covered with bare corkboards that bore the pockmarks of long- term use. On one of these boards there was a notice. *New Staff* it read and beside each name was a desk allocation – Jonathon Downton, C12.

John studied each desk he passed as he navigated his way to his own. Except for the colour of the plastic laptop cases, there appeared to be no discernible difference from one to the next. The chairs were black, swivel models without arm rests. The desks were veneered, cherry finishes with plastic silver pots stuck in the top right-hand corner containing a meagre set of stationary equipment. Under each desk was a set of metal drawers. Pairs of cubicles shared a waste paper basket.

John located C12 and sat. From the echoes of footsteps and murmuring he considered there to be four or five others in the room, but from within the realms of the cubicle it was difficult to tell where sound originated from. In the top drawer he found seven boxes of paper clips, five boxes of miniature Scotch tape, eighteen highlighters (each a unique colour), three pairs of scissors, a box of pencils, a compass and a heap of chalk stubs. In the middle drawer there was a high visibility jacket still inside its packaging. There were four deflated miniature footballs, three staplers and an A4 pad with a single sheet remaining. The final drawer contained a considerable amount of dust forming into clumps within the crevices. On the verge of lifting the lid of the laptop, someone clearing their throat made him pause.

'Hello.'

'Hello,' John replied, the chair serving its intended purpose, allowing him to face the woman. She was bohemian; sporting flared trousers, glasses and hair she didn't know what to do with. She slapped her clipboard against her leg and trailed her finger down the list.

'Darren Newton?' she asked, hopefully.

'No, Johnathon Downton. I read the chart on the wall over...' he span this way and that '...there,' he concluded, waving his hand in a large circle.

'Hmmm. Yes. No. Well, that one appears to be outdated. This is now reserved for Post-Primary science. It is noted that you are now allocated D18.'

'Oh, sorry about that,' John said, rising to slide the chair under the desk.

'No need to apologise. Mistakes will be made early on,' the woman replied jovially. 'See you later,' she added, pointing John in the right direction.

The desk at D18 could have been teleported from C12. They had even left the single sheet of paper out. At least John couldn't remember returning it to the drawer. The laptop was already plugged into the mains and the screen was developing a warm ghostly fuzz as it warmed up. John ruled a line down the centre of the paper. On the left column he started his list: English, Maths, History, Geography. He was then interrupted by a man halfway through a sandwich. The opening comment was muffled by the bread, but it sounded like "hey up".

The man was dressed in a salmon polo shirt, stretched at the stomach, with a branded symbol on the breast pocket John had never encountered before. He resembled a character from a *Wallace and Gromit* short. He took another bite of his sandwich, waiting for an explanation.

'I'm John. A woman with glasses and untamed hair directed me here as she said the forms on the walls had been updated.'

The man tilted his head back as if ready to accept this, but rather than bring his chin level again he shook his head and swallowed, his gelled grey hair unwavering.

'I'm sorry Johnny, this is AJ's desk, has been ever since it was set down and will be for at least the next couple of years, see,' he said, turning the sheet so as to point at his initials in the top corner above a carefully sketched trophy. 'That's going to be mine this year,' he added, prodding the drawing like a bully prodding a weedy child's chest. 'AJ, tennis champion. I'm going to have it engraved. Sit it right here. Polish it daily,' he continued, though such musings had spilled out unintentionally and he quickly returned to the matter of his unexpected guest.

'So you said it was Ryan who directed you here?'

'Err, no, a woman,' John began.

'Yeah it's okay, she's called Ryan or rather she's known as Ryan. Her real name's Rosemary. Don't ask why it's not Rose or Rosie. It is what it is. Anyway, let's check this one out, they may have updated it,' AJ said, leading John to another corkboard, his right arm gently swinging as if he were in the middle of applying topspin.

'Jonathon, Jonathon, Jonathon. Here you are. Primary right? B8.'

'You ever feel like you're part of some large-scale game of Battleships?'

'Ha! All the time. Listen, you need anything just come and find AJ,' AJ said, leaving John with a pat on the shoulder as he whistled his way back to his desk.

John found row B and made his way down it, knowing the woman heading in the opposite direction was also going to rendezvous at his alleged desk. She reached it before him and waited to the side. She was a local girl with a pleasant smile and simple black attire.

'Mr Jonathon,' she said, greeting him with her dainty hand protruding fractionally from her waist.

'Hello,' John replied, supposing his plight had been mentioned to someone in the administrative department.

'I'm here to help you set up as requested.'

'Oh, right, just let me open my laptop then,' he said, finding at this stage that the stationary pot was not stocked at all. He pointed this out but the woman shook her head and explained that she dealt with IT issues only.

'Procurement,' he repeated, about to ask where this room was located, when the woman tapped the monitor.

'Username; first four letters of your first name, last four of your surname. Password; lyon123.'

'Any capitals?'

'No.'

When he pressed enter, the little box shook to show access had been denied.

'Fingers must have slipped,' John said, hitting each key with his index finger only to receive the same negative judder. Behind him the woman appeared far from impressed.

'JOHN,' she said, leaning in, watching him punch the keys one after the other.

'R.'

'R? My surname's Downton.'

'Dougherton, no?' the woman said, revolving her clipboard. 'You wrote to me and told me to meet you here twenty minutes ago.'

'No, I didn't write. I've been down here for…' John checked his watch as he rose at least eight inches taller than the woman, who like all the local female staff wore plain black heels. 'An hour now. I've been moved around countless times and all I want to do is get on with some work and set myself up. Can we do that since the other Jonathon doesn't seem to be here right now? Can we find my desk and computer? Can you help me, Jonathon Downton, set up?'

The woman carefully examined her paper and flipped it over, scrutinising every name until she reached the end.

'No,' she said, 'you're not on the list.' And without another word, she took her leave.

11.

John's level of frustration was reaching the point where the only way in which it would suitably subside were if he vented through a verbal bludgeoning. He decided to find Margaret in the hope of avoiding this, expecting the person responsible for him being there could explain precisely what sort of pact he had entered into.

Marching up to the first person he encountered in the corridor, and in order to prevent them from slinking by as if he didn't exist, he demanded to know where her office was located. The man, wearing grey overalls and an oversized visitor's badge the size of a hardback novel, opened his eyes in fright and began apologising profusely for his actions. He dropped his toolbox with a clang in order to clasp his hands together and then repeatedly fingered the badge, the weight of which was placing an obvious strain on his neck. Attempting to subdue the reaction by waving his hand didn't help matters as the worker appeared to mistake this for not being good enough and was quickly down on his knees.

'Get up! What are you doing? No, don't do that,' John pleaded, trying to pull the maintenance worker up by the lapel, as he twisted his own neck back and forth to make sure no one else was bearing witness to the incident. Thankfully, by the time the door at the far end of the corridor swung open, the man was on his feet.

'Getting to know the locals?' Ron asked, wearing a three-piece topped off by a fedora in a deep matching charcoal.

'Are you supposed to wear hats inside?'

'Pardon?'

'Nothing, just trying to explain to my man here that it was my mistake, not his,' John said, patting the worker on the shoulder as he scurried off to start the job he had been called to attend.

'And what else?' Ron asked, jerking his head to suggest John was best to follow him.

'I was also trying to find Margaret Gillies to ascertain just what I'm meant to be doing here,' John replied, as they veered left through a miniature corridor which extended all of three paces and into a large U shaped room. At the end were two units, one in the process of being gutted.

'Step into my office,' Ron said, sliding through the door, blinds already drawn. He had started the process of giving his space some individuality. There were photograph frames of family members on his desk and a framed cowboy hat on the opposite wall which was dusty and torn and squeezed tight against the polished glass. A brass plaque beneath claimed it had been worn by Billy the Kid.

'Seriously?' John asked, holding his breath as he went within an inch of the glass, the brown felt frayed and on the verge of withering into dust around the fine edge of the brim.

'That's what it says. Carbon dating analysis concurs with the timeframe. Obviously there's no receipt and there's no photograph of him in it, but from buyer to buyer it can be traced back. You want a drink?' Ron opened a miniature fridge packed with carbonated cans.

'Coke please,' John replied, twisting to catch the can, still stationed in front of the frame. 'What type of hat is it? Have you seen the original receipts? When is he supposed to have worn it? Sorry, I mean there's so many questions.'

Ron positioned himself in his reclining chair, clasping his hands behind his head, his Sprite unopened and perspiring on a coaster.

'That's its purpose. It's a bowler. They were what cowboys usually wore since it's an extremely stable hat. It won't blow off whilst riding a horse and famously it endures a good stamping. The person I received it from had a booklet, a couple of receipts, verified stories of its origins dating to March 1878. Lincoln County.'

'That's amazing,' John stated, finally taking one of the three seats on offer on the opposite side of the desk. He'd almost drained his can. 'Tastes so much better when it's cold,' he said, 'like some fabled empowering elixir.'

'One of the first successful franchising operations in America - Coca-Cola. Pemberton licensed selected people to bottle and sell it in 1886. The bottling's still franchised per country. That's why it tastes slightly different across the globe. I'm a Sprite man myself,' Ron said, tapping the top of the can lightly. 'Used to drink lemonade but the last time I tried it the dry bitter taste left me coughing for hours. I have a friend back home who's the opposite and tells me he couldn't touch Sprite as it's thicker than syrup,' Ron concluded, shaking his head dismissively at such an opinion. He finally popped open his can.

'So,' John asked, leaning forward to check the door was closed, 'how have you been finding the place?'

A smile was there, though it was absent from Ron's lips: 'People have been telling me stories. I hear a new one every couple of hours. Carl told me half of you hadn't been informed of how the school operates.' John nodded slowly. 'Listen, from my perspective it's brilliant. Do you know how easy it is to entice prospective parents with the words innovative, ground-breaking, dynamic and ultra-safe when you already have a brand name synonymous with academic heritage and success? It's so easy I'm already being passed documents and tasks outside of my jurisdiction to deal with.'

'Well, at least you've been able to get yourself started. I went down to try and sort my workspace and it would have been easier locating the Hanging Gardens. I was about to go and search for Margaret to establish some answers,' John said, glancing down twice in the direction of the fridge.

'I wouldn't bother. She's so elusive it's like she lives and breathes within the realm of another dimension. It's the same with the rest of the Senior Authoritative Leadership Staff and Management Members. If you want to reach them the only way is email.'

'Is that part of their lack of direct interfacing policy?'

'Could be. Only time will tell I guess. Anyway, I'm going to have to shoot, I've another meeting in five. One for the road?'

12.

On this occasion, John was the first inside the Designated Primary Meeting and Discussion Space. He had loitered in the corridor for a couple of minutes suspecting he had misread the schedule list, but being ten minutes early, had concluded that if he was supposed to be elsewhere, someone would come and collect him.

Having not taken the time to analyse the room yesterday, John could now see how it had once functioned as a classroom. There was a grubby rectangle on the wall where a whiteboard had once hung. Dark blotches where Blu Tack had been were sporadically dotted on each wall. String hung limply, tied to the plasterboard tiles in the roof. A laminated pyramid was half hidden behind the desk showing expected levels of punctuation.

Five minutes before the meeting was due to start, others began to drift in. The small ginger girl entered sporting a dour expression. It was at odds with the beaming smile her companion wore, who despite being in the midst of a monologue, broke it off to state she hoped John was having a good day.

'Likewise,' John replied, as Carl strode towards him with a pallid complexion, the after-effects of a late night.

'I came by at eight and rang your bell. Knocked a couple of times too,' he said, removing one of three bottles of water from his rucksack.

'Must have been when I'd gone out for groceries round the back,' John lied, knowing he had been asleep. His decision to lie down for ten minutes after returning from a run had transformed into ten hours.

'We're off to the same place on Saturday. I'll let you know what's happening once everything's confirmed.'

John asked what it had been like as he watched three men (who he assumed were those missing from yesterday – Craft, Shaft and Latte) whispering conspiratorially to one another. The one in the middle was dressed for a business lunch. His tie was lacquered down inside his waistcoat and his hair stood rigid two inches from his scalp. To his left was the traditional teacher in corduroy trousers looking perennially bored. The final man was rake thin and showed no signs of overheating in his cable knit sweater despite the air-conditioning being out of service.

'From what I could tell from the bus trip, it's its own unique suburb. Could have been a borough of London I guess, except the prices didn't make you start you searching the net for home brew recipes. Very cosmopolitan. Everyone spoke some level of English. There were draft beers, cocktails, tapas, pub grub, whatever's your bag really.'

'Sound great. Take long to get there?' John asked, as the man dressed ready for Wall Street consulted his watch and cleared his throat.

'Twenty, twenty-five minutes.'

'Good morning everyone. For those of you new to Lyonton, I'm Trevor Shaft, Head of Pastoral Learning and Nurturing Care in the Primary Learning Phase. Mrs Welk and Miss Pond apologise for their delay but they will be here shortly. In the meantime does anyone have any questions?'

'Yeah, hi, sorry. Bearing in mind that we are due to start tomorrow, when are we going to be given daily timetables, curriculum overviews, a calendar of events, those types of things?'

'A good question,' Shaft replied, flicking through his pile of documentation. 'I suspect Mrs Welk will want to go through all that when she arrives.'

'Hi, yeah, we were just discussing last night what the implications for assessment were what with the fact the children complete all their tasks from satellite locations?'

Neither Craft nor Latte showed any inclination to involve themselves in the discussion. The one in the sweater had gently pushed his chair back so that it propped against the wall, allowing him to rock on the rear legs whilst his hands cradled his head.

'Sorry, what do you mean exactly?' Shaft asked, his suit clearly custom made, conforming to each of his contours. It was a crushed blue and offset by his claret tie.

'Well clearly we're incapable of seeing exactly who's completing each task we send. Mum, Dad, grandparents, tutors could all be aiding. They could simply type the question into a search engine to look for answers. I mean surely there's been a dramatic rise in one hundred percent test scores since the implementation of this digital delivery system?'

As he was speaking, John had watched Shaft nod along in agreement and he looked as though he was about to concur that such a method was skewing all their data and making a mockery of the day to day set tasks. However, he instead paused long enough to reply,

'Anything to do with the academic learning process is best to be explained by Mrs Welk and Miss Pond. However, I will say that this year I have managed to secure each child a packet of colouring crayons in the stationary pack they receive at the beginning of the term. Anyone...' A couple of people went to speak over the top of each other, whilst a few hands had also crept up.

'...oh, would you look at that. There's Mrs Welk and Miss Pond,' Shaft added, taking his seat, making everyone turn to face the open double doors where nobody presently stood. Faint footsteps could be heard and in response to inquisitive stares, Shaft nodded that what he had stated was indeed true.

'Is this being filmed? Carl whispered, as a woman made tall by a pair of three inch heels finally appeared in the doorway beside a large cardboard cut-out of a tree that was walking itself.

'Hello everyone and what a pleasure it is to finally meet you all,' Welk announced, flushed red, slightly out of breath, hair neither blonde nor brunette. She was American with the gait of Bambi. She flashed her immaculate set of teeth as she nodded this way and that, her body a series of sharp points.

As the tree followed it became apparent from the shards of bark breaking off that it wasn't compromised solely of cardboard. Peeking out from the side so as to weave her way to where Mrs Welk had positioned herself in the centre of the room, they were also introduced to the doll sized Miss Pond. If the children were in the building she would have been dwarfed by those ten and above. She carefully propped the tree on a chair and made her way over to join Shaft, Craft and Latte, her roll of the eyes meant only for them.

'So,' Welk announced, clapping softly, taking her position to the rear of the tree which had deposited a small mound of soil. 'We were all supposed to be introduced yesterday but due to our work on the Decision Tree, we took the decision,' she paused momentarily, 'to delay that until we were satisfied with what we had to show. Now, as you may be able to see, it is still a work in progress. As you can definitely see, our desire to produce for you an organic entity has paid off.' Shaft and co. stared directly ahead, each producing nods so vague it was hard to tell if the movement wasn't simply due to an intake of breath.

'The reason we hadn't completed the tree yesterday was not just because we wanted to collect and use natural materials,' Welk said, her voice soft and her smile coming on unprovoked at every pause. 'But because we thought, okay, usually a decision tree starts from the top down through the green leaves because we view the top as coming to a point, a hierarchy,' she continued, using her arms to demonstrate. 'But what is the most important part of the tree? What is it that nourishes the tree? Provides it with goodness? In this case, knowledge that allows it to grow and blossom? To reach high up into the sky like a towering sequoia? That's right, the roots. These are what keeps the tree sturdy and give it balance. If you will, it is akin to the foundations of a house, without which we couldn't have the rest of the structure.'

At this stage she removed a black notepad from the pocket of her jacket to scribe notes. 'Obviously, although we would all appreciate this marvellous creation on our desks, that isn't practical. So a paper copy has been included for you to consult in the back of The Staff Guidance and Assistance Handbook Edition 75 that Kate is going to provide you with. Now, does anyone have any questions regarding this?'

'Err, yeah,' Carl began, as a document thudded down onto their table.

'Good job I didn't try to catch that, I'd have broken my fingers,' John muttered, as Carl continued.

'I always thought the purpose of such a chart or document was to very easily define the flow of power up to a single point; a line, or pyramid, of responsibility with the apex occurring because of simple numerics. For example, in football: players, coaching staff, manager. Our base would of course be our children, who like the club's supporters, could also be deemed the most important aspect. Without them there would be no support to prop up anything above. I mean, technically, this establishment could run without Mr Sugarman, but wouldn't without enrolled students.'

Despite the majority of murmured agreement, it was Trevor's wince that caught John's eye. Mrs Welk's lips had formed a pinched O.

'Interesting,' she remarked finally, as a smile grander than before emerged. 'And what is your name, sorry?' she asked, reaching for the black notebook. 'Carl? Excellent, great, well I'm sure we can return to this another time. For now let us all focus on The Staff Guidance and Assistance Handbook Edition 75. If you turn to the front page you'll find the contents: Mission Statement Page 4, Dress Code Pages 5-8, Marking Policy Page 9, Disciplinary Procedures Pages 10-15...'

'She isn't seriously going to read the whole document,' Carl whispered, not the only one leaning across to mutter to their closest colleague. John scanned the room to ascertain whether they had anyone on the staff who was blind.

'Maybe she's having it notarised?'

13

John sat in the lunch hall staring out towards the kitchen. Numbed. Listening for two straight hours to procedures had induced a coma-like state he was struggling to escape from. He doubted anyone had remained focussed beyond the verbatim reading of the contents page. At one point he found he had turned ten pages, as he was coaxed out of his torpor and drawn back into the clarity and meaning of words, but had no recollection of what had been said within that timeframe. By the culmination of the opening fifty pages, his body was much like that of a car whose battery had been left on overnight. The calories burnt from maintaining a position that wasn't horizontal had been replenished by a large bowl of rice and shredded chicken.

He sat contemplating the purpose of reading the document word for word and arrived at nothing plausible, especially given the fact they each now owned a copy. Had someone once questioned her literacy competency? Was it a test of endurance for a forthcoming role in *Henry V*? Was she undercover CIA testing new torture techniques? What his body craved was a jolt of energy from either a couple of laps on a treadmill or a fizzy drink. Unfortunately, having wound down the whole allotted break time at the table, John was unable to provide it with either and instead trudged his way to the Educational Curriculum Transfer Hall.

With light filtering down from the series of mezzanines and people visibly bustling between work spaces, the hall had shrunk, though it had lost none of its inhospitable edge. The slogans that were hung in the main theatre were now also visible on corkboards in the corners of the room.

With no guide at the door, nor any of those in the Leadership Team evident, John headed to his original seat to await further instruction. The laptop had been opened, but aside from that the space didn't appear to be hosting anyone. He sat, rocking in the chair, peering out, awaiting a presence to shift him elsewhere. When this didn't occur with immediate effect, he nudged the laptop, mindlessly striking a couple of keys, waking the device from a mild slumber. *Welcome Jonathon Downton.*

The message was displayed inside a dark square. John clicked on it and it disappeared, leaving the background wallpaper which was the aerial shot of the building and grounds.

'Well this is fantastic.'

John's arms shot to his side as he started his explanation.

'I was…oh, Mr Sugarman,' he said, standing to greet the head. At close quarters he wasn't as gargantuan as he had appeared on the podium. A fraction under John's six foot, he was still an imposing presence, his body that of a rugby forward's going to waste.

'Managed to locate your space. Already have your laptop up and running. It's always encouraging to see people taking initiative. Not too much mind,' he added, John uncertain whether this was said in jest, or if not, how he was best to respond.

'It's always good to be in the, well, classroom, where the real action is.'

'Hmmm,' Mr Sugarman replied. 'That is one form of thought. What is most important is that you are on-board with our practice and ethos and why would you be here if you weren't?' With John having no idea as to how to reply this time, it became rhetorical. 'Excellent, I shall leave you to return to your duties then,' Mr Sugarman added, taking leave, his head moving in the mechanical fashion of an owl as he continued his observations along the column.

John sat, his email icon glowing red. Twenty emails. The first was from ICT telling him they had set it up. The next was a class list with email accounts. Third was a teacher in the Post-Primary Section announcing one of their pupils had lost a purse. The email after was the same teacher stating all was well as it had been located behind a sofa cushion at home. A curriculum list from Miss Pond. A note welcoming everyone in the Primary section sent to the whole school from Mrs Welk. A message from Mrs Welk forwarding a digital copy of TSGUA Handbook Edition 76. A message from Mrs Welk forwarding on the digital copy with it actually attached. One of his new parents asking for homework. Another wanting to make an appointment to check on their child's progress. A letter from his health insurance with a three-page document of everything that wasn't included but could be purchased at an extra cost. A reminder from Serge regarding football on Friday afternoon. Then there came two goodbye notices from ancillary staff (sadly neither of which were written by Sundry, the attractive girl that had met them off the bus). John thought it a shame as both leavers had included their personal emails and numbers. Two statements that there were new positions available in Human Resources and Asset Assessments and two statements that these positions had been filled. The close proximity of these final emails could only mean that the new recruits were friends of friends or had been press-ganged from the surrounding streets having replied in the affirmative that they could understand English.

The opening block of English teaching was *Fact and Opinion*. Maths was always place value so as to gauge basic understanding of number, and the topic (which integrated Science and Humanities) was *Animals and their Classifications*. An internet search of animal facts brought up a page on flightless birds, which would work well as a preliminary piece to gauge the understanding and ability of the class. John copied it and began editing the language to a suitable level, then again to a basic one so there were three variations of the text. Underneath he typed his own paragraph.

Are penguins the coolest birds of them all? I mean look at the way they slide across the ice. It would be so much more fun if you could move from place to place by throwing yourself along the ground on your stomachs. The only problem is that I think the white patch down the middle of the penguin is due to the black hair being rubbed off.

He then wrote six tasks into the body of the email the work was attached to and hit send. Next he moved onto his A4 paper to scribble ideas and plans for the forthcoming three weeks of work surrounding the subjects he'd been prescribed.

When he glanced up at the screen again, his inbox flashed red with a message stating it had been unable to fulfil the send request. *Our*

'What the? Bloody Jesus,' John spluttered, jumping from the chair, ready to hit delete as if that would solve the problem. He expected klaxons, armed personnel and newspaper headlines demanding a ten year minimum sentence. An ankle bracelet that sent forty volts through him if he wandered within three hundred metres of a school. His search history would exonerate him. There had obviously been a mistake. He leant over and scrolled to see if it detailed the lines of inappropriate content. Sure enough, in his opinion section, the words *birds* and *rubbing off* had been highlighted in fluorescent yellow.

Unplugging the laptop with his heart steadily regaining a regular beat, John made his way to ICT services. He forced himself to laugh at the issue, keeping his laptop at arm's length so no one suspected he was attempting to hide evidence.

'Hello? Hello.' The room was open plan with screens filled with numbers and statistics running on each wall. One was for the weather and another filled with binary. At the front counter there were wires, speakers and components of all shapes and sizes awaiting attention. Behind it were five unmanned desks.

'Hello? ICT folk, hello?' John called again, searching for a bell or a buzzer hidden under the tangled collection of parts.

'Yes?'

'Ah, hello.' The woman arrived from behind him. She was short with glasses. A local. Someone who read code for pleasure.

'My name's John, I...'

'I am on my lunch break,' the woman announced, taking her place at the rear desk.

'Right. For how long? Is there anyone else in the department around?'

'For three and a half minutes. I do not know where my other colleagues are. It is not their designated lunch hour,' the woman replied, her fingers a blur across the keyboard.

'In that case I'll wait here until your break's over,' John said, leaning against a glass panel that looked suspiciously like it belonged to a squash court. He brought out his phone to pass the time, cradling the laptop in the crook of his arm. Five minutes went by. A light cough achieved nothing.

'Hi, sorry, excuse me, has your break finished now?'

'It was over one minute and fifty seconds ago,' the woman replied, staring at him blankly. 'I have been waiting for your email. I have nothing from you in my inbox.'

'Well, no, I haven't emailed you. You might have seen one regarding me though, which is why I came straight here with my laptop.'

The woman wasn't satisfied.

'Err, my name's Jonathon Downton.'

'John?'

'Yes, John or Johnathon.'

'Ah.'

'Yes, so you received an email about me sending something pornographic?'

The woman nodded, her hearing impeccable.

'Right,' John continued, his volume resuming a normal level again. 'Well I came to show you the mistake the computer had made so that the document could be sent again and any such record of me sending that sort of material could be completely and utterly wiped from any system.'

The woman suddenly paused her typing: 'The computer made a mistake?'

'Yes, of course,' John said, turning the laptop to face her. 'It's misinterpreted the words, taken them out of context.' The woman remained doubtful. 'Aren't you going to look at it?'

'You haven't made a request.'

'Pardon?' John said, pushed up against the counter. 'I am in the midst of making a request. **"Aren't you going to look at it?"** is a request. Sorry, I mean *please can you?* I wasn't being rude. It's just that I really want to have it sorted as soon as possible. It's not something that you want hanging over you in your inaugural week. Or any week for that matter.'

'Any issues concerning electrical equipment within the premises of the main building or any buildings associated with the Lyonton group, within the confines of the greater Gebjin area, must be directed via an electronic request to the ICT department,' the woman quoted, ready to continue with the next paragraph when John raised his hand.

'Right, but I'm sure that you'll take into account my apprehension of sending another email, especially about the content. That's why I came to see you in person?'

'You cannot send an email to me?' the woman asked, roused into standing.

'No, my email works, I mean I suppose it does, I haven't actually been able to send anything since the one email I tried to send bounced and alleged I'd committed an offence that I certainly haven't. Could we just assume my email isn't working? I mean I'm assuming the protocol about emailing to register the problem is so that it doesn't get forgotten or that there's a record so that if anything goes majorly wrong there's some accountability. However, right now there is not a queue of people and since you didn't race over to sort this collection of equipment on the desk, I'm also going to assume you're not under some imminent deadline to fix it. So would you please kindly help me out?'

'If in the event of a fault to your laptop, desktop or other device, you are unable to register online with the ICT department, you can fill in a paper copy of your issue. These are located in the HRA office.'

John pinched the bridge of his nose.

'Why would you put...you know what, it doesn't matter. Just give me a second,' he said, double-checking the address he had typed in with that on the laminated card on the wall. The woman returned to her desk, wiggled her mouse and allowed her fingers to do their job. A minute later, John received an emailed response.

'Dear Jonathon, having read the content I have been able to clear the record stating that an attempt was made to send

unsuitable material. The issue surrounding your emails is that the safety settings have been calibrated to the highest setting. I would send you a list of words not to be used, however, as this wouldn't send, this is not possible.
Kind Regards,
Joyce

'Sorry Joyce, what you're telling me is…' Joyce raised her head, lowered it to the screen and then back again to John. 'You want me to stand here and email?' Joyce didn't answer. She didn't need to.

'Is there any way you can change the extreme nature of the settings so that banned words are allowed in the correct context? If not, it's going to prove very difficult for me to deliver tasks.'

Pressing send only brought forth further resentment to the laptop and system he found himself in. On this occasion *extreme* and *banned* were highlighted. 'Do you know what Joyce, I'm going to leave my laptop here and I'm going to find someone with the authority to switch the settings to a reasonable level. Then you can change it,' John said, depositing it beside her. Joyce blinked at him as she processed what was happening.

'But,' she said, stopping him as he headed beyond the glass door, 'how will I email you when it is ready to collect?'

14.

'Do you want a beer?'

'Only if it's a really cold one,' John said, as he stepped inside Carl's flat. He had been one of the few not to take up the offer of a bus trip to the local markets on the weekend. For those new members desperate to create some semblance of a home, however, they had returned laden and straining with goods. Three rugs, a welcome mat, inoffensive framed pieces of art, scented candles and a beanbag were what Carl had added to the basic furnishings they had been provided with. Two miniature speakers delivered low-level pop songs in the kitchen away from the eight guests who sat in the lounge. Ron was there in a trilby, so too was the ginger-haired girl, Fergie and her smiling North American friend, Catherine. The rest John was unacquainted with.

'How's the day been?'

'Don't ask,' John replied, examining the label on the bottle.

'Can't have been worse than mine,' Carl said, remaining in the kitchen.

'What do you mean?'

'Welk ordered me in for a meeting. Soon as I reached my desk I open my laptop and there's an email. She didn't say anything to me after the reading of the handbook and I passed her in the lunch hall twice, not a word. I get into her office and she starts telling me she has a problem with my attitude and that if I don't agree on how the organisation is run I'm best to leave now.'

'And what did you say?' John asked, the filtering of the pale yellow liquid through his teeth doing nothing to improve the taste.

'I was so taken aback I didn't know what to say. I told her I wasn't sure what she was referring to. Then she went on the attack and told me I knew exactly what I'd said and that my body language showed a clear lack of respect. I was going to point out there were people yawning and almost prostrate across the tables by the end, but I didn't want to drop anyone else in it. Then, just as I'm about to leave, she brings out the handbook and reads all six pages dedicated to disciplinary policies and procedures. I'm just glad she had her head down when I rolled my eyes or I'd have probably been sacked.'

John's tribulations seemed petty in comparison, though he still detailed them all. He explained that for the past two hours since leaving Joyce he had unsuccessfully searched for anyone who had the words *assistant* or *head* or *deputy* or all three in their titles to overturn such ludicrous settings. Eventually he had stumbled into Kate the secretary, who had informed him they were in various meetings and the best way to make sure they received any message was via email. She then enquired why he hadn't responded to her electronic invitation about the one at 0730 tomorrow morning. John asked her where else he would be at that time and with timid confusion her reply had been simply to question if he was accepting or rejecting.

Rather than continue their anti-social stance, Carl and John rejoined the others in the lounge as the ringing doorbell preceded the pizza delivery man. Although famished from spending hours plodding Lyonton's corridors, John held back from grabbing at a box.

'You not hungry?'

The girl who'd spoken dropped to the beanbag beside him which secured itself tight against her dainty frame. She drew her knees together to create a safe platform for the box, steam rising as she flicked open the lid, her hands nimbly selecting two slices, one of which she flipped on top of the other. She nodded to the box as she opened wide.

'Tuck in.'

John leant forward, leg pressing against the firm edge of the beanbag, the visible seam straining. Her circular eyes followed his hand.

'Thank you.'

The girl chewed, her cherub cheeks flexing. She could have passed for a final year secondary student were it not for the faint creases in the olive skin at the corner of her eyes. A girl who enjoyed late evenings but knew the importance of an early morning.

'I don't believe we've met,' John said, eating at a more reasonable rate than he usually would, while the girl snapped at her double-decker slice. One second it was there, the next it was not.

'We haven't. I didn't arrive with you,' she said, this time selecting a singular slice, a smudge of tomato sauce at the edge of her lips.

John hesitantly pointed it out and her tongue massaged it in a slow, circular motion.

'Thanks,' she said, rewarding him by sliding the box in his direction. 'My name's Catrina. I'm something something Primary Educator with something. Who are you and what do you do?'

The day's incongruity vanished.

'Ha! Yes, I'm doing the same as you. They have to reduce the font for the title to such a degree to fit it on paper that I've only ever heard it. My name's John.'

'And your purpose here is to save money and pick up local girls?'

'Why, is that what you're here to do?'

Now Catrina laughed: 'Could be. Sorry, I shouldn't assume. It was just when I was hauling my suitcase off the belt, a guy says from behind "here, let me help" reaches past, presents it to me with a heroic smile and then, after looking at me properly goes "oh, you're white" and walks off.'

'Well, it beats being told that you have a couple of gay friends who would be interested.'

'Or that you're a paedophile.'

'Yeah, the latter is more of an unspoken thing, thankfully.'

Catrina pointed to the final slice, which though rightfully John's, he ceded. In return, she sacrificed her comfort to create enough space for him to join her on the beanbag.

'So if it's not money and chicks you're here for, what is it? Discovering yourself? Escaping? Please don't tell me, especially after what I've been hearing from everyone else, that it was "career development" you were after? Oh, and incidentally, I do have a couple of male friends who would definitely be interested.' John sought an answer. 'Oh my god, it's the career development isn't it?' I'm sorry.'

'No, I'd never say I'd gone anywhere to develop. It sounds like I sit in a dark room all evening processing and analysing everything that's happened. Do people work in such a calculated manner? I suppose some do, but in coming here was I expecting to "grow" and my professional development be nurtured? I don't know, maybe, not really. I was drawn by the name, the badge. Lured if you will by the exotic aspect. In terms of the academic side, if I'm comparing it to my school at home, it feels like I've traded a room with a view for an unlit labyrinth. What about you?'

'Opportunity to travel to otherwise far flung destinations during the holidays,' Catrina said, her attempt to stand forcing them both to their feet. John followed her to the fridge, acquiescing on the offer of a second beer.

'A slightly more simplistic reason,' he admitted, awarded a look down her top as she crouched to gather drink from the bottom shelf, loitering there in the cold air.

'I had a friend who I worked with for five years. An Australian. Lovely. But she had this desperation for a baby. On her thirty-first birthday she announced she was heading home to settle down. I asked her if they had some ranch outside of Perth filled with eligible and willing men in their thirties. She claimed that she'd been looking in the wrong place for the past five years, yet I'm sure people in Camden, Angel and Chalk Farm do marry. Although maybe she's right, maybe she will meet a like-minded person, they do tend to congregate in similar circles, don't they?'

'You mean we're alike?' John asked, forced to lean against the wall with the beanbag having been appropriated by Carl and Fergie. He caught Ron's eye as he did, the man sitting comfortably, observing, his body language forever non-threatening, an intermediary between conversations. John was surprised there wasn't a queue of women ready to take him home to introduce to their parents.

'Let's see. If you can name six countries beginning with C and ending in A, you can take me home and fuck me.'

'China, Cambodia, Canada,' John blurted. Catrina read his forthcoming question and answered in the affirmative. 'Costa Rica, Cuba and…' She drank like she ate. She returned from depositing the bottle in the bin, took his hand and said, 'Croatia, let's go.'

15.

Unlike their prior meetings, the Wednesday Primary weekly morning briefing was not held in the former classroom, but in a subterranean bunker that had once been used for storage. Comfortable chairs, art deco settees, a coffee machine and a few posters stolen from local university dorms did little to subjugate the feeling it had once been used for torture. The ceiling was low enough to induce anyone above six foot into stooping or craning their neck.

When they arrived, Mr Sugarman was already seated on one of the settees, coffee mug in hand, three-quarter length coat open as though the lair were his own living room and he was preparing to leave for work. Though he gently nodded to those who found a space anywhere except either side of him, he said nothing. There was hardly any discourse apart from a couple of "good mornings" and a few gentle nods. John stood behind Carl, watching people glance from face to face, each passing moment feeling as though this was the one when somebody opened the session, but those who were in a position to do so looked across at each other with subtle gestures that implied it wasn't their   turn.

Catrina had entered with a Starbucks' coffee mug wearing attire that suggested she had failed to make it home last night, when in fact she had. She looked at John, twisted her head from side to side and shrugged. Mr Sugarman removed his glasses to inspect the lens and returned them. There was a sniff, a dry cough. Mr Shaft took a larger intake of breath than usual, but what followed was further anticipation that what they had come for was about to begin.

The spell was broken by a clattering down the stairs as Mrs Welk fell into the room at full speed.

'Uh! Wow, there you are,' she announced, as though she had stumbled upon a carelessly planned birthday surprise. John watched as she claimed an inability to locate her laptop had been the cause of today's lack of tardiness, as well as needing the right shoes.

From what John could tell thus far, it appeared she had retained the dress-up box she'd had as a child and used it on a pick 'n' mix rotation. Today's leather jacket complimented a floor length sky blue box pleated skirt. She took a seat next to Mr Sugarman, who remained like a commuter, hands folded across his stomach.

'Well, the reason I brought us here today is because it is a Wednesday and Wednesday mornings will be a time for us all to gather together and discuss what has both happened since the previous Wednesday, and what will be leading up to the next one. For example, we may discuss whole school events or I might inform you that members of the board will be coming for inspections. There are many reasons for us to have this briefing and it works really well to give a clearer picture and understanding of what we will be doing.'

Carmen, the perpetually smiling brunette and companion of Fergie, raised her hand.

'We still have a staff meeting on Monday afternoons though, right?'

'Oh yes, of course! Yes, Mondays are for extended meetings to discuss curriculum and operations and that is when we can go into full-scale detail. Here and now, Wednesdays, these are for the titbits, the reminders, the dust pan and brush to Monday's vacuum as it were.' Her black notebook was open on her knees and at this stage she made a scribbling. 'If Mr Shaft or Miss Pond or Mr Craft or Mr Latte have anything, they'll regale us with their important news, but they don't have any today. At least I don't think they do. Oh you do? Goes to show I should ask beforehand.' John stared at Mr Sugarman the way a corner man does a ringside doctor.

'Yes, so I just wanted to let you all know I'll be emailing out the extra-curricular duty list. Write your name in at least two boxes and I'll finalise it tomorrow,' Mr Shaft said, passing on to Miss Pond who explained she would also be emailing them with details of where to save work and planning. Craft and Latte both passed.

'In that case our first Wednesday meeting comes to a conclusion. Don't worry, all of this has been minuted and will be with you, if and when you need it refreshing, by the time you reach your desks.'

Having reached his terminus, Mr Sugarman stood, gave Mrs Welk an approving nod and headed to the sink. John raced out to catch Jenny in the corridor.

'It's not always like that is it?'

'Nope, usually lasts ten minutes longer,' she said, walking purposefully, arms swinging.

'But why didn't they tell us all that yesterday? Surely it would have been easier for everyone to send an email since there wasn't actually anything to talk about. And why talk about sending an email, rather than just sending it? Is there some sort of verbal quota they've to fill each meeting?'

Jenny strode, without response, until they rounded the corner, at which point she abruptly halted, stepped to the side and pinned John against the wall.

'Look,' she said, licking her lips. 'There are a couple of phrases that don't work here at Lyonton. One of them is "surely" and the other is "you'd assume". When you catch yourself about to mutter them, don't, or you'll start to lose the plot.'

'So we turn up, sit down, listen and leave?' John asked, edging forward from the wall.

'You heard what happened to your friend Carl yesterday. Last year we had a girl who was sacked after three months and no one knows why. I heard about five different rumours from good sources and they spread through the department and school as they do. Suddenly we're all called into a meeting to be told not to listen to, or disseminate rumours, except there's no explanation or context given. The incident in question isn't mentioned at all. It was like it was a hypothetical scenario.'

'And there's nobody to talk to?'

Jenny opened her laptop to check the time.

'Keep walking or we're going to be late. Listen, this is a franchise, a business, a money making scheme. The real Lyonton, the one established centuries ago that has espoused world leaders and Olympic athletes, they lend their name on the basis of a fixed fee and an unsullied name. They hold us at arm's length like a bastard child, not that the students or their parents are aware of this, or for that matter new staff. Beneath those in the stony walls of Britain are the shareholders. There is no local authority or union out here to go crying to, ultimately the people at the very top take quarterly stock of spreadsheets and if everything is in the black, and barring some calamitous tabloid headline of abuse, then that means this place is being well run. And inside here? It's like an interconnected spider web. You tell something to Pond, you might as well go to Sugarman. He appointed them to their positions, he backs them. If you become tangled with one, you're either going to be devoured alive or you're forced to cut yourself into freefall. All the time people are conscious of references and having to please those above and yet you want to inform your future employer they're not worth the paper they're written on.

'Don't get me wrong, there are some great educators here, people whose opinions are valuable, and yet due to the fact they don't have a title, no one cares. It's like being in 1970 and despite having Mandela to vouch for you, all anyone wants to know is what Nixon thinks.'

They crossed the threshold of the Educational Curriculum Transfer Hall together.

'This all sounds very bleak,' John said, conscious of eyes following them from the mezzanine as they traversed the narrow columns of the booths.

'Why do you think you are one of thirty new staff? You want my best advice? Do yourself a favour and think like a shareholder,' Jenny said, her final comment before she slid out of sight.

John slumped at his desk and blinked. There was a chance it had been the diatribe of an embittered employee, an anomaly who had been overlooked for promotion, who had recently been told there was no revenue left to reward her with an expected raise. However, considering it was the money keeping her in the position, he guessed not. What she said made sense, the silence in the meetings thus far verified the culture Jenny claimed reigned.

Time is Money. Show me the Bottom Line. What are our Forecasts?

Shareholder's thoughts were of no use. John started to compartmentalise the weeks and days until the first holiday as he brought up his new barrage of emails. The first was from Joyce informing him he could collect his laptop. Another explained his gas and electricity meters would be read when it was convenient for him. Four hours later the same person explained it had been done and thanked him for his cooperation.

For the children's work, he had regurgitated the documents that had been used by the teacher of the class last year. It had him thinking like a shareholder and considering whether a robot couldn't be programmed to replace all the staff. Robots could send out the next sheets using an algorithm having determined the child's success on the paper it had previously sent out. There surely had to be a way of programming it to generate its own sheets, raising or lowering the difficulty so that each child's needs were individually met. That would be truly revolutionary and something that could be patented – he could already see the board members ordering themselves a new fleet of cars.

John opened the recently sent document from Shaft that came with a spreadsheet attached: Origami, Story Time, Music to Dance to, Interactive Chess, Interactive Scrabble, Physical Sports (on-site, must be willing to travel to other schools for competitions). John typed his name into this final box and replied without filling in a second choice in the hope of stealing a lead on others who would be interested. He then regretted not adding information regarding his qualifications for such a role, which he guessed would automatically be distributed within the PE department first.

Two of the emails had arrived from students showing they had completed their worksheets, but neither of them had achieved full marks, so John informed them to look more carefully over the numbers of those questions they had failed. After that he sent a message to his whole class enquiring whether they required any help and, receiving nothing after a couple of minutes, excused himself for a toilet break.

It was at the urinal where John became acquainted with the man Serge had spoken to him about whose title was presented as an acronym that could have passed for a Welsh village. His shorts were of the running variety with a half-split seam, though they were cotton not polyester. His shoulders were thick and rounded, pressing forward in front of his chest. The socks he wore were crumpled around his ankles and John was surprised to note he was wearing trainers rather than studded boots.

'Hi sorry, are you the HOAA, err, the line manager of Serge?' The goatee was there, a prominent tuft jutting out from under his lower lip. There was a scowl too, but that might have been due to John's attempt to converse rather than silently staring ahead at the tiled wall as etiquette dictated.

'That's me. Why?' the man said, shaking himself twice.

'I just have a couple of questions,' John said, tensing in the hope of speeding himself up. 'I'm in primary and I've had an email about extra-curricular activities and it says the children here actually do physical practice and compete in competitions. Is that true?'

The head nodded: 'Why?'

'I was wanting to know what my chances of being appointed were? I assumed that members of your department would be given first choice, what with it being their area of expertise, but I do have a range of coaching badges,' John offered, drying his hands on a paper towel whilst the head left his unwashed. His days of playing rugby or wrestling had given rise to consider hygiene feminine.

'I've no problem with it. My department tend to focus on the theoretical side.'

'Right,' John said, following him, the man moving at a hobble, on the brink of stumbling every few steps.

'So does that have something to do with the lack of a running track? It said on the form that the people taking the children must be willing to travel to other schools,' John said, feeling like a journalist. Watching the Head twitch, he thought he may have posed one question too many. He expected him to begin ranting or tell him to ask someone else, but as they entered the section of booths dedicated to sport or (Physical Exercise and Theoretical Tactical Accumulations of Mind, Body and Spirit), the man calmed.

'You know, I reckon I'm glad you asked me and you're not hearing some ludicrous chaff from someone else. When it was being built, these whole grounds, from scratch, I'd drawn up a four hundred-metre track. Eight lanes. Polyurethane. When we came to the final stages: groundwork, tractors in, materials, Sugarman comes to me and says that having spoken with the board, with the vision of the school, the way it's moving towards a revolutionary, decentralised, non-invasive approach, we could save massive amounts of money. Children don't need to *do* or *participate,* they can follow or learn by watching clips. Look how popular and effective consoles like Wii have been in generating an interest in sport. So we agreed to decommission it and the funds went into the marketing department.'

'But the problem was that none of the other schools shared this ethos?' John said, sneaking peaks into the booths, which had been widened in order to accommodate the members of the department, three of whom were hulking women spilling off their seats. John doubted they could jog, let alone participate in a recreational activity other than bingo.

'Precisely. It's to their detriment of course, but you can't educate prawns. The staff here know how to crunch data better than anyone in the Northern hemisphere. Stats, records, diagrams, video clips. They are able to provide the most detailed information any aspiring sports star would need. See the learning statements up on the walls? Well we have our own in this department – *The Sporting Theory of Everything.*'

16.

Two and a half days into the first term and John calculated that having mastered locating and distributing previous year's work that would pass the censors, he worked ten minutes per sixty-minute lesson. Having dedicated time in the evening to sorting files into folders, he estimated he was a day away from having everything prepared up until the Christmas break. What he was now attempting to work out, was how to stave off boredom for the forthcoming fourteen weeks, which were split by a single week's holiday he had yet to book. Web sites were either restricted or monitored, and using his allocated free slots per day (when children took specialist subjects such as music or PE) for casual reading, he was ready to join them in learning the local language.

The prospect of football at the culmination of the working week kept the horizon bright, and indeed past four 'o' clock, he had spent ample time in the gym and pool. Plus he and Ron had already enjoyed a game of badminton, providing a healthy workout for them both.

With one of his free periods occurring before lunch on Friday, John had taken himself down to eat ten minutes early and had been sitting between conversations for the past five minutes. They revolved around excessive workloads, misinformation and aspirations for the weekend. He was ready to return to the solemn life of the booth when Carl caught him. From the crimson cheeks and clenched fists, John assumed he'd been reprimanded for another trivial comment or action, but on this occasion it wasn't only him who was affected.

'A meeting?' John repeated. 'After school today? Seriously? It's the weekend, there's football on.'

'I'd brought my kit bag and placed it under my desk. I'm sure it's been organised because she spotted me carrying it.'

'What the hell is so important it needs to be delivered on a Friday afternoon? You'd think if it was that significant she could have done it now.'

'"It won't take longer than an hour. It is information that will benefit the whole educational community within the primary sector."'

'The only person benefitting from it is her husband.'

As the working week reached its culmination and most of the staff from the ground floor to the many mezzanines were lifted on the current that the weekend's sanctuary brought, John and those in the primary section trudged from their booths with either an air of acceptance or begrudging, each as visibly obvious as the next. John stared at Jenny as he leaned against the wall and watched her shake her head and wag her finger in tandem.

In terms of money spent for recruitment purposes, was it worth keeping the staff happy and retaining them for prolonged periods or were advertisement and convention centre costs negligible when you took into consideration that those who remained moved up the salary scale? Was that a question the shareholders regularly asked themselves?

'Well hello, look at all of you here,' Welk announced, adhering to her time management MO. She was in a fight with the bags she had tangled around her neck, coming across like a comedian performing a routine. 'So,' she added, forced to tilt at the waist and wrestle the straps over her head. 'Myself and the rest of the Leadership Team for the Combined Phases of Primary and Early Years Section, really thought that what we have to tell you couldn't wait.' From behind her there were a couple of shakes of the head. Craft appeared to have mastered sleeping with his eyes open.

'We have been reviewing the safety settings policy for the past two years and we have now decided that, as a move throughout the department, we will be lowering the restriction settings with retrospective analysis of sent documents to be performed instead. This decision has not been taken lightly. We have sat and discussed the merits of the present system for many months, however...' a tap of her jacket pockets revealed they were empty of the little black book. She had no luck under her shirt either. 'I knew I should have prepared a PowerPoint,' she muttered, hands roaming to her jacket once again.

'Are some of the facts,' John ventured, 'that parents of siblings are asking why work never changes and the date on some papers is three or four years old? That some facts are out of date: *President Obama, The News of the World Reported.* That sheets are either too difficult or too simplistic?'

Welk's eyes narrowed; 'what makes you say such things?'

'Just a hunch,' John said, watching her mentally scrawl in her black book, as those around the room looked anywhere but at the pair of them, pretending to have been momentarily distracted.

'In the end, there were cons that outweighed the pros. It was long, calculated research that led us to this,' Welk assured the room. 'What we're always thinking of is how can we best address our Elevated Learning and Collective Collaboration? So now I am going to go through the twenty-six step guide of what to do to activate the process of downgrading the security settings. As this has been forwarded to me as an email, first you need to have your laptop. Secondly, you need to book an appointment via email with Joyce, the Assistant Head of Electronic Communications and Maintenance, Sub Division Two. Thirdly...'

Carl slunk in his chair so the dots kicking a ball on the horizon passed out of sight: 'Cunt,' he mumbled, agonisingly coherently.

At the conclusion of the twenty-sixth point, the torpor that had taken hold left many unable to do more than drag themselves from the room. Those who had been playing football outside were still doing so, but at a reserved pace. By the time he had walked home and changed, John sighed and resigned himself to another session at the gym when he came upon Catrina waving him her way, blocking off his doorway.

'Hey stranger. Had you been planning on joining the boys for a game of football?'

'Yeah,' John replied, exhaling slowly.

'Well, you do know there are different ways to exercise don't you?' Catrina added, shoulder and hip resting against the wall. 'Come on,' she continued, offering her hand, 'this time we'll go to mine. I have toys we can play with.'

There was a thin film of sweat. A sign of achievement. A symbol of longevity. A mark of satisfaction. John remembered being fourteen and asking of the internet, the collective minds of the world, "How long should sex last?" The amount of comedic ripostes told him he wasn't going to be given a straight answer, although there had to be some scientist who had attempted to boil it down to a formula, a number of precise seconds that split the difference between a medal and a lifetime of obscurity.

'Until you're both satisfied,' he would tell his younger self, who would go away unsatisfied by such ambiguity. His current self refrained from asking Catrina if she was. Instead he gently stroked the side of her breast; the movement drawing her closer to him.

'How would you describe me?'

'Spontaneous.' John paused there. *Sexual, attractive, relaxed, fit,* he thought.

'I'm not trying to trip you up, I just want to hear the vocabulary you use.'

'You're athletic, sporting athletic, trim, fit, toned,' John said, emphasising the final word, which would have sufficed on its own had it come to him first. He sought to provide further flattery but found that clichéd superlatives for beauty didn't suffice and he didn't want to come across corny. The substitutions he formulated sounded even more hackneyed.

'The stalling isn't because you're hideous and I have a *Pinocchio* problem, it's just I can't identify the exact words I need. You'll have to give me a couple of minutes,' John added, draping a leg over both of hers.

'Don't worry, there's no rush. Let me tell you what I've been thinking about over the past couple of days during our foray into remote teaching. I was sat there yesterday and I opened my drawers and there wasn't more than a dozen items in them. At home those would have been so full that as soon as I reached for the handle, goods would have been spilling out. Drawing pins (twelve boxes of them), scissors that had been there since 1975, boxes of glue sticks and spreaders, rolls of border tape, split pins upon split pins lying at the bottom like I was holding a lucky dip. How much does that save them per annum? Then there's all the equipment in the classrooms: whiteboards, smartboards, pens, pencils, sand timers. I had three sand timers: one minute, five minutes and ten minutes.'

John nodded. He enjoyed listening to her and wanted to hear more. There was nothing extreme – she was neither harsh nor delicate. She was ph 6.5, not bland, cool, soothing, crystal clear stream water. She was assured. She had a purpose. She did what she wanted. None of that was contrary. He would tell her that.

'If I ever wanted the children to do anything on time, I'd use them. Forget clocks or digital timers. I'd tip the sand over and there it was for all to see. Time passing. A precise amount. A physical shifting from the present and future to the past. You try to teach them about minutes, to and past. Teach them to understand timetables and they struggle on gradually, but you place a timer down and there it is. Either more time left to run or time nearly out. You know Death, The Grim Reaper, he's never gone digital. The measure is there, exact. The time stored. The hourglass glued into place on the shelf with no resets or pauses. Can you imagine seeing what has gone and what is left? The measure of what remains compared to what has already been?'

And there John had been thinking how fate was accidental, that the sand could slip through in any order. That the only things that were clear in life were when the opening grains dropped and the final grains trickled out. That what was hidden between those minuscule pebbles of sand, as they sluggishly caved in, was chaos itself.

'Why do you think those first creators chose that figure, the hourglass?'

'Is it not something to do with infinity? It would resemble the infinity symbol on its side, but it probably isn't. It must be due to the speed or the ratio. Maybe it was due to the way the glass is blown, the rounded top and bottom forcing it to be held in an outer wooden casing to hold it sturdy.'

'You don't think it has anything to do with women?' Catrina asked, the question inviting a long look down her body: trim, tight, pert, supple. 'Not this woman, the classic woman, Venus. The wide-hipped, child-bearing mother who starts time anew.'

'I would have thought it was the other way round. An "hourglass figure" suggests someone made the connection to the body later and idealised the image. I can't see how it could be another shape and work. It's like the wheel, perfectly designed.'

She had started to trace the image on his torso, her fingernail scoring the skin as she altered the size of her motion and moved slowly south. Infinity. Definitely infinity. Looping again and again and again. She walked her fingers, fine drips of sand rhythmically falling.

'Tell me, what do you have left?'

As Friday was a day with no extracurricular activities and the fields were sublet on Monday and Wednesday (first to farmers who sold their produce using weights so worn they had been reduced to smooth metal nubs that no longer carried numbers, and secondly to a yoga group consisting of one female instructor and one man who wandered freely with a lyre through ye gruppe of however many women there were, serenading them individually with a gentle plucking and spoken word), on Tuesday and Thursday, from three to five, the pitches were crammed.

On the first occasion John had gone outside to coach his team, he had assumed Shaft had forgotten to tell him there was a youth carnival on. Smaller children weaved their way through the older students playing games of tag, whilst senior students stood in larger groups, socialising in a manner they would usually do at lunchtime.

'I thought I had the pitch,' John said, having managed to locate two footballs (only one of which was the correct size), eight cones (six plus two Caution Wet Floor signs) and eight bibs that were three different colours all in XXXL. He had altered his original plans for the session as soon as he had entered the equipment store, but now Plan B was equally as preposterous.

'You have,' the Head of Athletics and Sporting Teams Structured Development announced, standing in military fashion, casting watch over his domain. 'It's marked out here for you in red cones,' he added, pointing to a five by ten metre grid.

'But I thought I had the first team, the under nineteen boys.'

'Oh you do. The under nineteen girls will be beside you. Then we have the under sixteen boy's athletics there and the under fourteen girl's cricket there,' he said, finger rising as he explained away every space leading towards the fence, until they became no larger than two by two. 'Tends to be vertical jumping rather than high jumping there obviously, but a similar technique is adopted. Ms Boxin will talk them through it for half of each session, bring out her whiteboard, draw out the steps, walk it through in a kind of circle. Of course all this helps our safeguarding policy. No adult is ever out of ear shot and eye sight of five or six others and just in case, every coach wears one of these,' he continued, picking up a fluorescent jacket. 'Bought the batch in XXXL just so they would definitely fit everyone rather than having to order new stock every time the staff changes. There's some safety pins in the box by the side if you need them.'

'But what about equipment?' John asked, the jacket sliding from his shoulders.

'We tend to hope they'll bring their own.'

'And the space? Twenty-two players in fifty squared metres?'

More coaches had started to appear. They were tucking their jackets inside their shorts and using the arm-holes for their heads. They were clipped in with so many safety pins they jangled. By the time they had found their allocated spot on the field it appeared as though older children had dressed in adult jackets to play make-believe construction-site.

'Don't worry, space isn't something to concern yourself about,' the HOAASTSD said, becoming visibly irritated by the questioning. He marched out into the melee in order to distance himself from John as much as to ordain proceedings. Rather than blow the whistle that sat against his barrel chest, he barked "right" as he clapped his dry, abrasive hands which had the desired effect on those nearest to him. However, on the fringes, the games continued. He bellowed thrice more until everyone had been immobilised.

'Finally. Thank you,' he announced, beginning to pace lines between the cones. 'Everyone here knows the rules. Those of you who aren't in full kit, and I mean full kit, are to make laps around the outside for the duration of the session.'

A couple of the children raised their hands.

'Tough. No excuses. Let's go. Hurry it along,' he concluded, his job for the day done.

With no cap on the numbers, and even with four of his team being side-lined for being without a fully logoed Lyonton kit, John was still forced to send groups of twelve out at a time on fitness laps which tended to be only slightly more than a walk due to the volume of traffic. By the end of the forty-five minutes he had spent as much time tossing back quoits and kicking away balls as he had done coaching. It was hard to tell what anyone had achieved apart from setting foot outside for some fresh air and practicing their manners as they excused their encroachment on another's space.

John caught up with Serge, who was one of only two from the five PE staff to have coached.

'Hey, has it always been like that?'

Serge nodded, bowling a tennis ball against a lamppost.

'But surely…you'd assume…why don't they change the time of the market and yoga?'

'You don't want to go there,' Serge replied, chewing the raw, pink skin around his nails. 'You ask about switching times and the only people who'll be staying later are us.'

'But it's our facility, they just hire it. They aren't the ones in charge,' John moaned, guided towards the sports hall by Serge who nodded sympathetically and gave him a reassuring pat.

'I'm sorry, think like a shareholder, I know, I know,' John said, as they began setting up a badminton court.

'What?'

'Oh, it's what Jenny told me to do so I wouldn't become frustrated.'

Serge tilted his head, lips pursing and pouting as he stretched.

'It's not a bad idea I suppose. This one could have been avoided mind. Legend has it that when it came to signing these contracts, rather than pay an agency or a bilingual local to translate, they did it through Google Translate. It transpired only after they'd been hastily signed by the outside groups, that rather than just a two month lease over the summer holidays, they were allowed the option of choosing to renew the lease every two months. Therefore, barring famine or some recreational and vegetable medical report by Andrew Wakefield, they're here to stay.'

18.

John and Carl walked shoulder to shoulder. They had moved in such fashion since the moment they'd stepped out into the shadows cast by the quad for the start of a new Wednesday morning. Had anyone asked John who the taller of them was, he would have sworn it was himself, yet each time they were together, his friend proved to have half an inch on him.

'Guess where I was yesterday in the period prior to lunch,' Carl said, strutting with his bag slung over one shoulder. During the first few weeks he had regularly used an electric razor to maintain a certain amount of shadow, but for the past fortnight he had left his beard unattended. The rugged hair was now full of curls and the patches on his neck were thicker than elsewhere. A full moon would shortly be gracing the sky.

'Again? What for this time? I don't think you've spoken in a meeting since,' John said, squinting as the sun greeted their arrival on the road that circumnavigated the educational building.

'She allegedly works in the office on the floor above. She could call down to me if she wished but she doesn't even have the courtesy to email me. She gets Kate to do it.

'So there I am in the middle of a lesson, sending notes to correct the picture of the whiteboard work I've been sent, when I'm emailed to say she wants to see me now. I reply that I'm currently teaching and can do lunch or straight after, but no, a response is sent to me twenty seconds later informing me it has to be immediately. Up I go and there's Welk sitting in the middle with Pond and Shaft flanking her like theatrical decorations as though I've been summoned to a court marshalling.'

They were in the building now. The corridors were empty except for cleaners mopping away in their green shirts.

'She tells me I know why I'm there and I stare at her in the identical blank fashion Pond and Shaft are at me. I thought about asking whether I needed a lawyer present. "Yesterday," she says, "you rolled your eyes in the meeting." I told myself I wouldn't say anything but I just blurted out "Sorry? What? When?". It was halfway through her reading the PowerPoint on emergency procedures apparently. I wanted to tell her I thought I had my eyes fully closed by that stage but instead I attempted, with total futility, to protest my innocence. The judge, jury and prosecutor has the audacity to tell me that I'm now wasting lesson time. Shaft fully flinched as I stood up. I guess he thought I was going to hit her.'

'What are you going to do?' John asked, as they took the concrete stairs to the basement.

'I don't know. We've only been here a month. My shipping hasn't even caught up with me yet. I mean I could go home and claim, well a vast number of reasons to future employees, but there isn't going to be a decent school with any positions open now, so it would likely mean subbing for a couple of months. Plus that ten percent annual bonus...'

Their gazes were in sync as they roved from the chairs to the wall clock then down to their respective watches. They were two minutes early.

'Well,' Welk stated, leaning forward, unable to look as imposing as she wished in a reclined position with her back against the settee. She kept herself rigid, the front of her shirt pushed up in an arch as though she had a second pair of breasts sandwiched between the original pair and her stomach. She sucked on the inside of her cheeks, her entire face cone shaped. 'Now everyone is finally here, I guess we can start.'

She bounced her folder against the table, the action all arms. She nodded at Pond who provided the laptop she had been typing at since she'd sat down. Since the very first meeting, John hadn't ever seen the Deputy Assistant Head of Formal Academic Learning Within Curriculum Hours without it and the reluctance to hand the device over was visible. As Welk rested it on her own knees, so Pond's fingers continued to type against her thighs as she edged forward to keep the monitor in view. John and Carl slunk to the side, the latter trying hard not to blink.

'It has come to the attention of myself and the Senior Leadership and Management Team of the Primary Sector that despite our request in one of the very first meetings we had, not a single person has followed our instructions to upload their planning, sheets, marking and resources onto the Sombrero System,' Welk said, turning the screen to the room, almost dragging Pond onto the floor. Her nail tapped twice on the Sombrero symbol which was located on the lower left on the bottom bar of everyone's laptop. 'Not one of you.'

'Weren't we told to place all of our work on Sky Cloud?' Carmen said, her hand raised a fraction above her shoulder. There were vague murmurs of agreement.

'I don't believe so. The Sombrero System is where work needs to be by the end of the week.'

Beside John, Carl's eyes were starting to water. John cleared his throat and said: 'But we were asked to upload to Sky Cloud. That's why everyone's work is there. I'm sure if someone opened their emails from that week's minutes they would find such a request.'

There was an automatic motion from Welk, Pond and Shaft to deny the statement, but the shaking never became more than a twist of the neck. Words were only mouthed consonants. Over to the side, Craft and Latte (had anyone been able to hear their conversation) were discussing the standard of non-league football.

Welk finally nodded as she brought out her little black book. A smile was breaking and her voice rising an octave.

'Mistakes will be made. All folders to be on the Sombrero System by six pm today. Happy Wednesday everyone!'

19.

Having learned new procedures and the names of people in the various offices, and with a clearer idea of who was who and with a rough idea of what they did (or at least what they were supposed to do) and having accepted that all drills for his football would be no more than three v three and that the children he took for it would bring in shiny new equipment the next session, John found himself settling into a routine. Rather than the weekly and monthly digital calendars resembling abandoned jigsaws, he was able to make sense of them at a brief scan and the days began to pass more or less as expected. Ad hoc meetings were constantly called to clarify points that had already been raised via email, but even these he had come to expect. The yearly calendar had been updated at least twice a week since he had arrived and it was now on its thirty-third version, which if anyone had taken the time to carefully analyse, was identical to the eighteenth.

Given a greater creative license, John had begun to receive longer pieces of work from his students. He could see the individuality arising from them. He could notice the breadth of their work increase. He couldn't actually see them, but he imagined them smiling, glued to the monitor awaiting their next task. Inside his cubicle he was left entirely to his own devices. Nobody ever popped their head in to see if he was there or what he was doing. No questions were asked of what he planned to do next or how he would do it, but then those in senior positions could, at a couple of clicks, view everything that had been sent and received from his computer.

He would often see Craft and Latte chatting, standing languidly in the space between their cubicles, shirt sleeves rolled to the elbows, swinging keys or rolling and unrolling paper, seemingly at a loss as what to do with their time. The other three were more elusive. Though they had desks on the upper mezzanines, broad desks behind which four or five people could have comfortably sat, they were never to be found there. Often there were traces of a recent appearance or disappearance: a water bottle, a jacket left on the rear of the chair, a document left with pages turned, but for the rest of the time they were at meetings or between meetings and judging by the emails they sent, they spent their time writing up what they discussed.

At first John had thought they wanted him to mark and assess their work as recounts, but now knowing any points would be repeated within a forty-eight-hour period for the whole department, he deleted them after the merest of cursory glances.

It was on a Tuesday, the day on which whole school leadership meetings ran from two to four pm, that John received an email from

Kate, the secretary, requesting his presence on behalf of Welk at 1530 in her room. It was the day John regularly played Ron at badminton. He was ready to email Kate back asking if she was certain about the time, but since her office was an antechamber of Welk's, he walked up and knocked on the door two minutes shy of his allotted time.

'Mrs. Welk is in a meeting,' Kate said, without looking up, hidden behind three stacks of paper.

'Is it the one she'll be having with me?' John asked, reading the Post-it on the nearest two-foot pile; *examples of planning to be properly triplicated – to file.*

'Ah, Mr Johnathon, yes, I know. Mrs Welk sends her apologies.'

'Was this as she simultaneously sent the request?'

'I err, don't...'

'Never mind. Yes, she has her usual meeting that she always has. So?'

'Yes. So she said, can you send her your timetable so she can pick a more convenient time?' The note on the second pile was signed P – *Haven't finished completing the tests, you know what to do.*

'But she already has my timetable. She asked everyone to send it at the start of the year. Look, it's here on the wall behind you,' John said, leaning across Kate's desk to prod the offending document.

'She says she wants it colour co-ordinated so she can tell which are your lessons and which are your free ones,' Kate replied, avoiding eye contact.

'Because she's unable to read? Isn't it she who decides what subjects we teach and which are specialists?'

Kate declined to answer. The third Post-it read; *Inform the stylist I'll be in my office 11-1. Will need Bollinger. TS* with a mark beside which could have been a kiss.

'Is this what you thought you'd signed up for?'

Kate stared blankly at him, like an animal at the vet, weary what the white coat meant, hoping he would pass on without further comment.

'It's okay, I'm not here to inform on you, we're just two people speaking. This room isn't bugged is it?'

Kate shook her head, hesitated, then shook it with more vigour. It was as if there was a black hole at the rear of her chair sucking her slowly in, diminishing her. John was now eager to stay for another five minutes to see whether she would disappear entirely.

'When you were younger, what did you dream of? It wasn't sitting behind piles of paper finishing projects your bosses couldn't be bothered to, was it?'

'A house,' Kate replied, free to elaborate when whatever retribution she feared didn't materialise. 'Red brick, two stories with a garage and two gardens, one just grass for my rabbit and the other with flowers and trees. An apple and a pear tree specifically.'

'And where are you with it?' John asked, certain if he persisted he would be presented with sketches of every room, the bed for the roses, the amount of windows.

'Well I always thought of it in England in a town with a square. So there, no, but here closer, each month a little closer.'

John refrained from asking how many years she had been uttering such a sentence or how many more she thought were required. He wondered what part of her target was completed for every paper she filed, every document she ghost-wrote?

Ron was already on court warming up in a grey tracksuit with a white headband low on his forehead. He jogged gently down the tramlines on his side of the net, pumping his knees high so they slapped against his hands. His cheeks puffed out. John swung his racket back and forth like a cutlass.

'Meeting?'

'Phantom one.'

'After a four hour one today I'll be dreaming of phantom ones tonight.'

'Four hours? What happened? You lock yourselves in? You weren't brokering a Middle Eastern peace treaty were you?'

'I'll see if I can condense it for you,' Ron said, pulling the post so as to remove the sag from the middle of the net. 'It started as a budget meeting. Bad news, our present outlay far exceeds what we're bringing in. People turn to me and I explain that we've recruited sixteen students since I arrived, which is up 152% from the same period last year. Sugarman sits there and says "obviously we're not doing enough". I agree, I've already broached him about how far behind we are in terms of marketing and how our current methods of flyers and letters are contradicting the futuristic message we are pushing in terms of the learning and the ethos for the students. However, for any changes to be made there would need to be a large initial outlay.'

John stopped him: 'Why don't they lay a couple of senior staff off? There's more managers in this place than there are in all the McDonald's worldwide. What they need is an abundance of low- level researchers finding texts, inputting data. Why don't they hire a financial consultant to come in? They wouldn't need more than ten minutes to save a quarter of a million.'

'Aside from the size of their fee, no one in that room is going to purchase their own rope. Apparently everyone is on rolling one or two year contracts, but from what I can tell it's closer in equivalence to The House of Lords,' Ron continued, removing his jumper. 'So the next question I'm asked is, how many students have we turned down since I started? Thirty-one. All of a sudden there's scoffing, arms being raised, heads shaken, mutterings of disgust. I read out the individual students and the reasons they were declined. When I accepted the job the remit I was given was that I always had to abide by the fact we are an English speaking educational facility and those who fell below the required level weren't to be accepted. They were to have it explained to them where improvements needed to be made, given the names of staff who could assist them as tutors and book another test date for three months' time. We want to maintain "the highest of calibres".

'But you see the problem is, as gifted as I am in what I do, there are the traditionalists who can't be swayed by the futuristic vision on offer. "My son/daughter is a keen sport's player and needs to be

practising four times a week and you don't even have a running track."
"Personal interface worked fine for the pair of us during our schooling, we want the same for our children."

'The fact is there are six other institutions of our size or larger competing in the same market. Plus with a couple of them, it isn't as if they are doing the traditional market well, they're doing it exceptionally – two sports halls, intervention groups, class sizes under twenty, international residential trips, etc. So back to the thirty-one declined,' Ron said, sweat patches already building in the arms of his t-shirt, a little tighter now than when he had originally purchased it.

'"Despite them not being able to speak English to the level we expect, the scores they are providing from their local schools are still high though?" Sugarman asks. In twelve instances this is the case - scores that compete with the elite of what we already have. However in terms of their English, it isn't a case of elocution or developing key scientific or geographical terms to enable them to write essays, these are students who are at the stage of learning the days of the week. They may very well have rote learned key phrases, alongside questions and answers in their specialist field, but at the point when I ask them what they did for their summer holidays, they merely smile, nod, bow and eventually respond, "Yes sir, enjoy school, I will try hard."

'So Sugarman sits and nods a while whilst everyone else does the same, as if they're musing as well as simultaneously admiring his musing, and then he says, "Well there is certainly no one here, or on the board, who wants us to change who we are. Our institution and education in English is what separates us from the local schools and was the primary reason for us being founded in this area. We have a brand and image to uphold and those at the original Lyonton who come for visits, to look at the books, to collect their donation and make sure their name is being sufficiently represented, are keen for us to maintain a profile which they feel represents them as an ideological, leading name in education. What we are going to do then is provide a set, standardised test for all entrants. We shall also hire locally qualified teachers across both Primary and Post-Primary stages. And to really hammer home the fact that nothing is changing I want, *At Lyonton we are an English Speaking School* below the motto on every official piece of paper." That's pretty much the speech verbatim. He excused himself to go to another meeting and left the rest of us to sift through the finer details.'

'So the test all new students are going to be given is…?' John asked, ready to start the game.

'The present entrance exam for Year One. And in order to adhere to the *everyone speaks English* slogan, all the new local hire will be contracted to a subsidiary company being created called Lyontone.'

'And what about the ancillary staff? Most of them only know the basics.'

'They've been told they can't speak once they're on the school grounds. If anyone from the original Lyonton questions their silence, we're going to explain they're all employed through a specialist mute recruitment centre and it's one of many ways in which we're continuing to boost our image with the local community,' Ron said, neatly folding his trousers onto a bench. 'Anyway, enough of that. I gave Carl a good beating at tennis yesterday,' he added. 'We tried to call on you but I guess you were resting up for today.'

John shrugged, the signal in the residency blocks was notoriously patchy.

'I had some work to do. I mean everyone always does, but you know sometimes you think it has to be done right there and then to make sure you're on top of everything. You push back the tide and once you start you suddenly realise that, rather than one or two items, there's twenty requiring your attention.'

'Carl was saying they want you to save everything in two separate places,' Ron remarked, hitting the shuttlecock cleanly, his action fluid. Each time they started his technique was crisp and then half an hour later he had nothing to give, firing stray shots with heavy steps and a tightening of the shoulder.

'They appear to fear some imminent internet apocalypse. They've Kate filing a third version in what's probably a lead lined cupboard. They told us on the first day to save everything to the Sky

Page and then last week asked why everyone wasn't up to date with uploading onto the Sombrero System. Carmen asked them if they didn't mean Sky Page and the whole of the ASLTT were adamant that they had never stated Sky Page to be the required destination. I asked why then, if that was the case, everyone in the room had saved everything to Sky Page and there had to be minutes of it somewhere. In fact, thinking about it, that will be what my personal meeting's about. Then yesterday we were informed that meeting minutes will now be delayed and sent out a week later so they can be checked for factual inaccuracies. We've been told that research has shown facts have a half-life, and I don't think she means "over a period of time" but more like half of what we read was false. No one asked the obvious. She removed her little black book shortly after. I'm beginning to wonder if she thinks she's some football manager, although I've never been able to fathom why they jot down notes because if it's important it should be stated right there and then. What are you going to do, head back into the changing room forty-five minutes later and recite from your musings having allowed whatever problem to exist for the past thirty?'

Ron nodded prior to removing his jumper. Any sport that didn't involve a racket was alien to him and he made no pretence otherwise.

Aside from asking each other if they were ready to start, and the cries of anguish and delight that punctuated lengthy or vital points, their conversation was held in stasis until the end of the match. At which point Ron accepted a sweaty hug with the same good grace he had done on the prior twelve occasions. Though this time, having run it closer than ever, he didn't mask his frustration.

'What disappoints me the most isn't getting beaten. It's the fact that I can see it coming and can't do anything to prevent it. Rather than picturing the point I'm playing, all I can see is the outcome. The toil. The stretch. The almost. I don't know where it comes from but as soon as we're halfway through that second set, no matter what the score, the losing mentality arrives. I try to suppress it and I say to myself, 'next point, all that matters is the next point'. I focus on that and meanwhile my conscious barges in looking decidedly glum. *You're going to tire.*

Losing it from a winning position shows a lack of heart. It's never *I'm three off winning the set*, it's *I'm seven off losing it.*'

'Don't worry, I knew that already. I can see it in your eyes,' John replied. 'Maybe give Nielsen and Smit a game. A couple of wins should give you some momentum and build false confidence.'

20.

On three more occasions, twice that week and one early the next, John's presence was requested by Welk. In the first two instances she was busy and on the third all Kate could do was shrug.

Since he had become accustomed to grabbing a sandwich from a deli counter and retiring to his desk during lunch to mark papers, John rarely saw others in his department outside of their near daily meetings. That meant that, aside from what he was told by Ron, Carl or Catrina, he was never privilege to any news before it was officially announced. Now, however, having sat himself amongst eight others who had less than five titles in their official role, he was treated to both their insights on his case and all the latest rumours.

In terms of Welk continuously missing his appointed slots, it transpired he wasn't the only one. On average it was calculated she made one in every four she organised. Those who had been under her command last year explained that they were told they'd be observed once a month, but come June not one of them had been seen. When someone had asked if these observations would be taking place in the final two weeks, she had informed the room that her position on the mezzanine allowed her to observe each of them daily and that, as an academic expert, that was all she required to pass judgement.

There was no hushed whispering as people disclosed information from around the table. Everyone spoke at a regular volume. Their freedom to divulge freely in disseminating all that they'd heard (95% of which would later be ratified officially) stemmed from the fact that management believed the hall was beneath them and took lunch in their offices, whilst within the dining area, just as with high school cliques, the staff stuck with their own kind, tables reserved in all but name.

On occasion, John had watched Sugarman pass through en route to another part of the building, his eyes shifting as he strode past the tables with files and folders secured between his hands and his chest. The volume in the room dimmed in his presence as though he were a Victorian schoolmaster and they were the juveniles vested upon him.

Despite what she had previously demanded of John, Jenny harboured the most bile and led the gossip. At each juncture she was unwilling to reveal her source, as if Deepthroat would disappear if she didn't adhere to the strict protocol set.

John sat and listened from the far end to the fact that one of the managers had left her husband to move in with a local woman. That Kelly, the short dumpy woman who had greeted them on their arrival, had also recently been sacked by Ursula who had hired her replacement and had the new recruit in working at Kelly's desk whilst she packed her personal items into a box. Tales about the budget deficit he had already heard. The reason there were fewer cleaners present on site he had not. According to Lucinda, a girl John imagined missed making daisy chains out in rolling meadows, the staff who had children were poaching the most competent ancillary staff to work as nannies. They were offered a weekly wage a third more than Lyonton was willing to provide them and this left numbers working in lime green shirts close to single digits. The final tit-bit before the culmination of lunch yet again came courtesy of Jenny.

'Sophie's told them she doesn't want the stress of responsibility of being Early Years and Foundation Overseer of Development Leading into the Primary Phase, so they're splitting the role. Now she'll only do mornings and there will also be an afternoon manager. Now, because legally they have to advertise every position, they placed one in the *Sucre Friday Gazette* (in case you're not sure where that is, it's a city in the South of Bolivia, population of three hundred thousand). It transpires that it's also a hub for foreigners learning Spanish. So despite whatever suspicions may have arisen over the ad being placed on a different continent, in a place with no logical connection linking it to our organisation, some woman out on an extended break, who just happens to be an outstanding Head of an Early Years in Newcastle, applies. They're flying her here for three days next week.'

The question was raised about the budget deficit and eyes were rolled.

'Perhaps they're paying her to do the cleaning as well?' John offered.

'That's all she's going to get. You know who the internal candidate is?' John understood that it was the one from their lowly ranks who was conspicuous by her absence. The flaxen-haired one who sat throughout each meeting without the slightest mutter or gesture. The one whom, if she had been at the table, would have been the cause for a whole different type of subject matter to be used as conversation. Though Mrs Brewer did not carry the same surname, she was in fact Sugarman's wife. John wondered what odds bookies would offer on the outcome of the result? Just as every other time he was privy to the inner workings and dealings of the organisation, he couldn't help but be bombarded by the obvious questions that must surely have arisen somewhere down the line of proceedings. Why hadn't they informed the outside candidate she wasn't what they were looking for with a standard pro forma? *We're sorry, but at this stage…?* Were they weighing the cost of the flights and hotel against points they were accumulating? Why hadn't they told Sophie it was all or nothing? Now they were going to have to pay for another full time role when Brewer went part time. Why, if they were forced to advertise, not do it in some dying language that was only spoken north of the Urals in some West African kid's comic? And finally, with a budget crisis apparently looming, wasn't this the perfect time to amalgamate two roles rather than expand one?

When he reached his computer, John found another meeting request. This one for 8pm that evening. He didn't bother responding and just set about working. The scheduling wasn't any inconvenience to his plans of thirty minutes in the gym and a similar amount of time in the pool. It even gave him time to go out and buy dinner.

Returning, post twilight, in jeans and a light jumper, headphones hugged around his neck, he found the corridors bathed in disinfectant. The remaining cleaners were keen to showcase their work ethic in order to gain their promotions. Most of the lights had been switched off except those by the doors. The doors were locked with thick chains except the single one he had entered through. When John had first been told those lights remained on to act as guides to the exits in case of a fire, he had assumed it was a joke. A couple of weeks later he had mentioned to Craft and Latte that maybe a set of bolt cutters should be placed behind the glass panelling next to the fire hoses "in case of emergency". They had said they would pass it on.

He had expected to reach the mezzanine to find Kate down to her final few papers, but her section was dark. Welk's office, on the other hand, was lit. John let himself in without knocking to find her with Shaft, who had assumed the position of court reporter.

'Mr Downton, you're finally here,' she said, emphasis on the modal adverb. In case Shaft hadn't recorded that she stared at him as he clunkily typed, striking the keys in a far less fluid fashion than Pond would have.

'Fifth time's a charm,' John replied, taking the only available seat, one from a camping store he had never before seen in the office.

'Mr Shaft will be transcribing throughout,' Welk said, her black book already open. She appeared ready to pick up the momentum when John withdrew his phone, placed it in front of him and pressed record.

'Just in case of any factual inaccuracies. A good way to cross check,' he said, leaning forward, signalling that she should continue.

'Well.' She moved her hands closer to her body as though she was afraid of becoming infected. Shaft was still typing. 'Let me ask you. Do you think learning should be fun?' She no longer directed the question at Shaft or John; she spoke to the phone. The screen had already gone blank, but it was listening.

'I think that would depend on a couple of things. The teacher and the subject,' John replied, his chair so low to the ground he was forced to look up. The view was supposed to intimidate him and give her a feeling of power.

For today's ensemble, including her fringe, everything had been cut sharply. The arms of her blouse and the legs of her trousers, both had been pushed through a guillotine and sliced. 'Although, I suppose rote learning times tables at a desk, chanting them and filling out paper would be boring, whereas going on a treasure hunt to match the question to the answer would be exciting. So maybe subject matter isn't important.'

'So you don't think excitement distracts from learning? How much time do you think would be wasted by searching for those numbers instead of reciting them? Do you propose transforming handwriting lessons into calligraphy ones so that more of the children "become engaged"?'

Shaft might as well have started playing games.

'Well I've never been able to understand the obsession with handwriting. Especially when as an institution we're so forward thinking and everything is done electronically using these apps and programmes. I'd say that as long as a piece is legible, I've no idea why it has to be joined. I mean, has anyone ever read work and thought, *you know what would make this a more calculated report* or *you know what would really give this story more intrigue and development — fluid handwriting*. If they have, they should be sent back to 1572.'

'So you don't agree with our procedures here?' Welk asked, pouncing forward.

'I don't believe that's what I said. Certainly no one has ever told me we have a handwriting drive.'

'But you have been told about the lack of interface, the measure of serious work. High expectations must be set by constantly delivering the message that this is work we are preparing students for. You have heard Mr Sugarman speak about the necessity for children to focus, to not be distracted, to see the work before them and nothing else. Going to a newspaper office to take your video of the process, to interview people and show them the machinery, is that not distracting them from writing their articles?'

'I suppose that depends on how you judge the importance of inspiration and whether you care about the end result. I could drive to the airport in a Ferrari, but I'd be better taking a taxi so my luggage fits.'

'Let me get to the point,' Welk stated, running her finger over her jottings until she located it. 'Here at Lyonton we have our four allotted days of fun scheduled throughout the year, spaced nice and evenly apart. An online fair. An online athletics gaming event. Another fair and.' She paused and glanced at Shaft who let her know three was all they had. 'Ah yes, no more digital pantomimes at Christmas, the holiday is too much of a distraction in itself. One per term. Enough fun and leisure for everyone. If these events occurred too often students would become blasé about them. Can you imagine having Christmas every day?'

'You'd be skint,' John offered.

'Exactly.'

'And people would be asking about the effects of the methane being produced by the reindeers. I'm surprised there haven't already been calls for Santa to outsource to a representative in each individual Christian country. Franchise if you will, dilute, in order to lessen the air miles. But with all the impersonators in the department stores doesn't he do that already to an extent? Is the suit and beard a sign of quality? Is it a symbol of trust across the world? An acknowledgement that you are going to receive the same service and benefit from the same ideals? That we're guaranteed that Santa experience? Or having been replicated from that one unique individual, does it leave those imposters as shadows? Copies that can never truly compete with the original. Does it matter? Are they not all one and the same or does the personality behind the beard count for more? Surely you can't have an identical set of people performing to such high expectations, there's too many boots to fill.'

Welk's eyes narrowed, not into slits, but horizontal boxes.

'I understand perfectly what you are insinuating,' she said, coiled.

'You do?' John replied, pulling the same look of confusion as Shaft. 'I thought I was nervously rambling. No wonder they say the author is dead,' he continued, beginning to look forward to receiving the ten page document if it was ever typed in full.

'Now let's see if you now fully understand me Jonathon. We both know that a tree's leaves are constantly pruned. Torn off and discarded throughout the life of a plant. But new ones grow in their place. Yet we hear constantly about the importance of having roots, maintaining roots, because they will be the ones that stay firmly rooted.'

'And yet,' John interrupted, not giving her the opportunity to dismiss him. 'If you find the plant to be healthy but you discover it to be full of too many roots and not enough soil to help it grow, you have to prune away those that are stunting it. Or if those leaves start to turn yellow or the plant is wilting it is root-bound and needs a sharp pair of shears to survive.'

Shaft had given up typing.

Very slowly, Welk closed her little black book and produced a glimmer of a smile.

'I will see you next week for a host of observations.'

'Great. No worries. Anything else?' John enquired, ready to push himself out of the chair, which were he to do so with too much power would collapse in on itself. 'Oh, do you want me to send you a copy of the recording?' he asked, directing the question at Shaft, the only person who acknowledged he was still a presence in the room. The Head of Pastoral Learning and Nurturing Care in the Primary Learning Phase tried to ascertain from Welk what her desire was, but her head had not altered from its position. Her chin was tucked into her neck, eyes boring down into her book.

'Err, you know what, let me get back to you on that. I'll email you either way.'

21.

Spending most of Saturday at a football tournament where he had watched his boys scrape through the group stage and then be walloped four-nil in the quarter-final, John hadn't planned to do much on his day off. As the games had been a preliminary test for a forthcoming and more prestigious tournament, he had attempted to analyse where improvements could be made. However, though he identified three key areas, without the space to coach it, such vulnerabilities weren't going to be addressed no matter how long he sat with his whiteboards and magnetic counters.

He had been dressed ready for the gym reading a chapter from *Blood Meridian* when the doorbell rang. He missed having a girlfriend, someone with whom he could discuss books, music and films. How many times did he write to the children reminding them to read with an adult so they could debate what had occurred? Wasn't that half the fun - regaling, sharing an experience and re-living it? If there had been English Literature classes in the upper school he would have visited one in a spare slot. As it were, with the lessons taking place in a chat room forum with students using abbreviated names alongside a host of emojis, it more closely resembled an online gaming site than serious literary discussion.

Those in the English department had once admonished the lack of punctuation and grammar of the replies they received that read like text messages to friends. The consensus had changed over the past two years though and they now stated this was the evolution of language. In order to write in such a bastardised form there first had to be a firm grounding in formal English. According to Jenny, the last two teachers of the subject had left after being told they couldn't replace Shakespeare with Tarantino and Coppola, because they "weren't adequately in keeping with Lyonton's image". One of the resignation notes had done the rounds on email before being systematically deleted.

'2 b progrsiv or stuk in da past that is da Q that no 1 in dis department haz an anser 2. I du not like dis place & cnt wast my time innit.'

John opened the door to Catrina, who had her finger raised ready to ring again. She was in vibrantly coloured yoga pants, hair loose, flowing in rough waves past her shoulders. Recently she had added highlights, subtle caramel ones that grew lighter at the tip.

'Are you coming to the spa with me?' she asked, a work of Thomas Pynchon jutting out of her hessian bag. 'I'm halfway through,' she said, bringing it out. 'Have you read it?'

'A couple of years ago,' John replied, back-tracking into his flat. 'What do you think?' he asked, racing around, shoving the necessary items into a bag.

'He makes me think of the novel in a whole new light.'

Half an hour later, with Pynchon's oeuvre still on the agenda, they took an escalator down into what, from the façade, resembled a failed motel. Down in its subterranean heart, however, they emerged into a giant underground prehistoric looking health spa. Between the pools of various heats stood trees and plants rising to the ceiling. Boulders leant into footpaths and in one corner the lights dimmed as the ceiling descended into a cave complete with stalagmites. Catrina led John to the outside area where individual pools were cut into the terraced rockery. She placed her book on the ground and threw her towel over it, then slid herself onto the furthest, tiled lounger. It was tilted at sixty degrees and half submerged beneath the warm water. She looked as though she was wearing nothing at all.

Completing their literary discourse they moved on to retelling their respective weeks. Catrina had set a half hour restriction of work talk as it seemed to be the only topic of conversation they had with anyone through the week.

With the latest major Primary debacle, the roles were, for the first time, reversed and it was John who was able to enlighten Catrina as to what had prompted the management's most recent declaration. On Thursday morning everyone in the primary department had received an email from Welk stating that – *from now on no meeting is to take place in a room with electronic devices as they cause too much distraction.* Simultaneously she had set up an impromptu meeting in the underground staff room for the following morning. Upon reaching the stairs to the subterranean room, however, she found all the staff situated outside it. An action that had been started by the local hire and which no one had any problem in following.

'Is it already being used?' Welk asked Pond, who shook her head, hoping that was as far as she was personally questioned.

'So what is the problem then?' Welk queried, squeezing through to find one of the Post-Primary Mathematical Excelling Educators pouring themselves a coffee. Welk turned to face those under her instruction more perplexed than before.

'Why aren't we going in?' she demanded, scanning faces for an answer before settling on Pond.

'Because of your directive,' Pond muttered, laptop and paperwork tucked under her arm.

'My what?' Welk asked, her bags beginning to weigh heavy on her shoulders.

'You said that no meetings were able to take place in a room with electronic devices,' Pond replied, knowing that as the one to have proofread the document, she would face the greatest wrath.

'But that's obviously not what I was referring to,' Welk said, any elegance she had been determined to portray in her chiffon dress undermined by the rapidly burgeoning sweat patches.

'If only they had been minuted,' someone said, the spokesperson allowed to remain anonymous as all kept rank.

'Well in that case...' Welk removed a bag from her shoulder ready to offload it, but Shaft, Pond, Craft and Latte all had their hands full and nobody else moved. It was hard to do so in any case packed in as tight as they were. 'It's a nice enough day, we'll do it out on the pitch.'

John located the button Catrina directed him to and transformed their unit into a jacuzzi.

'What are you smiling about?'

'Just thinking about the fact that as soon as Welk placed her bags on the grass, Shaft whispered that lessons were due to start and she was forced to email about the previous email as an explanation.'

John smirked as he rested his head, hands cupping it. He closed his eyes as the sun emerged from behind a cloud. There was uninterrupted blue sky all the way east.

'Okay, time's up on school,' Catrina said, playfully splashing his way. 'What would you care to discuss now? The English Premier League? Holiday plans? The state of the Middle East?'

'Let's start with the latter and work our way to the former,' John suggested, turning to the side, propping himself on his elbow, mirroring Catrina.

'And where should we begin? The annexation of Palestine? The dawn of Islam? The rift between the Sunnis and Shiites?'

'I was going to start with ISIS, they feel the most relevant,' John stated, forced to recline horizontally to set the bubbles in motion again. 'I'm just impressed by how high they aim. It's not like they've taken over a pre-existing country in a coup d'Etat, they've attempted to create a brand new state. Genghis Khan, Napoleon, you think these people are relics. You think their ideas to transform the land around them into one kingdom and redefine the boundaries are no longer feasible in our modern world. But there they are with swathes of land under their control and a recruitment system that puts to shame the world's leading organisations. I love how petty world leaders are about them too. Instead of going in and annihilating them, they decide to belittle their name "So Called Islamic State" "Un-Islamic State", it's like they believe they're on the playground again. Now, I am aware of the political ramifications of going to war in another's sovereign boundaries have changed over the past half a century, but you do think those countries, and indeed anyone who has suffered directly or otherwise from their rise, would briefly triumph a few White saviours?'

Catrina smiled and rolled back to face the sky: 'I had, or rather still have I think, a friend who thought the change of name from both the group itself and from those on the outside came across as very

Monty Python. He happened to be a web designer and, drawing inspiration from ISIS's social media campaign, set up his own page for The State of Islam. Primarily he attacked the Islamic State for splitting from the true path of The State of Islam, claiming that the identity of his group pre-dated theirs. He enlisted some guy who was studying Arabic to assist him in constructing the sentences in a similar style to IS. He created a manifesto with the first point being to reincorporate IS into SI. Then he designed a flag – white with four black swords boxing alleged writing. There was a message at the bottom in black that said only true believers of Islam could read what was written inside the swords. He posted pictures of IS members with grey in their beards stating that those with any colour other than black were treacherous and it was a symbol that they sympathised with the white west. There was only one white that could be tolerated. That was the burning heat of rage in the hearts of SI members that emitted from the flag into the eyes of the enemy.

'Where I thought he made a faux pax, bearing in mind his apparent desire for realism, was when he produced a women's fashion section that was just pages of pure black. The claim that even seeing women's clothes was haram.'

'And?' John asked.

'Do you know how many people wanted to make donations? Were asking where meetings took place? He was starting to think about producing merchandise. I suspect he would have made a fortune.'

'But some fun spoiling regulator shut him down?'

'No. Some cleric in Afghanistan put out a fatwa on him. I don't think he would have taken it seriously but when he tried to contact the student who'd helped him with the translations, he was told he'd gone missing. A housemate claimed he'd said he was going away for the weekend and never returned. His phone was turned off. He didn't respond to email. There was no notice given to anyone at the university or flat and the contact numbers and details he had given for relatives all turned out to be false.'

'Bloody hell,' John remarked, now sitting, stretching over his legs, the sun warming his back. 'So what did he do?'

'Depends on who you ask. He told me he'd bought a ticket to Russia and from there was going to take a train into Mongolia. Another of our friends heard he was off to Bolivia for a while. He could be hiding on a remote Scottish island or might be dining on road kill in Death Valley,' Catrina said, fixing her bikini bottoms as she stood.

'And the website?' John asked, following her lead back inside.

'He shut it down,' Catrina replied, leading him into the gloom where fake stalactites hung, blocking off the strips of light. They made murky the plunge pools that hid behind rising boulders. 'You know,' she continued, casting her towel to the ground before descending the stepping stones into the water. 'I came here in the first week and I'm sure most people suspect this section isn't in service,' she added, on her knees, tilting her chin to keep it above the water. Her eyelashes were matted. She pouted and the water rippled. As John took a step down, her hand emerged to tug at his shorts. 'I've been thinking about this since I woke. Why don't we see how long I can hold my breath?'

It wasn't that she could read his mind, it was that she could foresee his desires. Who wouldn't have wanted her in the pool right then staring up at them, luring them into the stinging warmth? It would have been simple to sit astride of him and pull the thread of her bikini to the side and gently rock in his lap. He had believed that would happen from the moment she had told him where they were going. Yet like on preceding occasions, she had superseded his expectations and shown him what he really desired, what he hadn't even dreamt to crave. She rose slowly, her actions controlled, her breathing regulated. She swept back her hair as she exhaled. John began to wonder how he had managed to go so many days without her.

'Twenty-four seconds,' she sighed disappointedly. 'Just let me rest here for a while,' she continued, pressing herself against him. 'And then we'll see if I can beat it.'

22.

After sitting to reflect on his practice with a more concerted focus, and with the promise of guerrilla observations looming, John wondered where Welk would stand. The cubicle wasn't large enough for a second seat, which would leave her upright for the whole hour. She'd be either pressed against his chair or up against a cubicle wall, which, being free-standing, had to be treated with the utmost care. Concluding she might observe from above with binoculars, John did, at least for the first week, gaze skyward at the start of each lesson in expectation of finding her sitting as though in the rear of the upper circle with a programme of study in her lap.

Now, a full three weeks later, John forgot that the threat of Welk's presence could be imminent. If the purpose of delaying her visit was to keep him on edge and in a heightened sense of apprehension, it was no longer working. John had now concluded she had either forgotten about him in the midst of the other shenanigans, or had more likely begun to form a dossier on him.

Those on her current watch-list included Carl, who walked around with such a wide grin it was only a matter of time before he was told, during one of his weekly improvement meetings, that his sardonic gesture had been added to his list of faults.

The other two she had placed on PIPs were the crèche teachers, the pair of whom spent at least two hours a day twiddling their thumbs whilst those in their charge napped. Their disagreement had apparently started over one of them typing too loudly, then escalated when the other had allegedly moved her cubicle wall one evening to claim three centimetres more territory. Rather than separating them by relocating one, Welk had, through Pond, ordered them to show civility and gain trust by taking their break and lunch together. As if that didn't go far enough, they had also been ordered to hold hands on the walk to and from the canteen to feel unity and develop an unbreakable bond. This latter requirement had been rescinded after three days, however, when one of them had gone beyond filing their nails into talons to taping drawing pins to their palms. The latest development had seen Shaft, Craft and Latte taking watch at a desk adjacent to theirs that blocked off the walkway. In passing John had suggested giving them both IPads so there was no noise from the bashing of keys and marking the floor with tape, so there could be no accusations of the cubicle's borders having been altered. Latte had said that he would pass it on, but that in their prior meeting, Welk, Shaft and Pond had been very upbeat about the effect their implemented plans were having and planned to continue with them for the rest of the term.

The sound of chairs moving signalled the beginning of lunch. John saved a couple of documents before pushing off from his desk and exiting. As he did he almost collided into Pond such was the close proximity she had chosen to wait outside the cubicle.

'Sorry about that,' he said, arching backwards from the hips, despite there being no chance of clashing heads when, in a pair of heels, she came level with his solar plexus.

'Where is your tie?'

John patted at his neck, top button undone. It was peculiar, he had followed his usual routine after waking. He'd showered, changed, had breakfast and there was no particular reason as to why this item of attire was missing. But it was.

'I'm guessing it's at home. I didn't even realise I hadn't put it on. It must have dropped from the back of the chair,' John replied, shuffling to the side a fraction as it became apparent Pond wasn't budging.

'You must wear a tie every day. It is written in the staff handbook edition 84.'

'I've no doubt about that. I'm assuming it was in edition 83 as well and I guess you're here as you want me to go home and grab it?'

'Do you not think a tie is necessary?'

'Well,' John started, glancing up to the mezzanine to see if anyone was making sure Pond was sticking verbatim to the script. 'Is that a personal question or a rhetorical one?' he continued, checking his watch. He only required ten minutes for lunch and his class had a PE lesson on the principles of basketball after that, containing an eight-minute highlight reel of LeBron James' finest moments. 'The modern necktie is descended from the cravat, which was introduced to Europe in the 17th century by a military unit, The Croats, a group as well known for their war crimes as their dress sense. It is believed, depending on who you read, that they wore their *Hrvati* for hygienic purposes or to close the top of their jackets. Now, as it doesn't serve either of these purposes in modern society, nor does it hide modesty, keep feet clean or stave off rain or sun when on the street, it could be argued it is defunct. An obsolete item that should have gone the same way as the hat did after JFK made it to power. For some reason, however, it has been placed upon a pedestal as a symbol of utmost propriety, despite the fact it's worn by politicians, lawyers and bankers. Many people would claim they look "smart" or "sophisticated". I assume there are people out there who would like to see the re-emergence of the shoe horn and quill and ink pots too, but are probably too weary of the internet to have a large enough platform to have their voices heard,' John said, wondering if he stepped to go round Pond she would mirror him to block off his exit.

'Mr Sugarman wants everyone to wear a tie.'

'By everyone you mean just the men though right, not yourself?'

'It helps the children work harder,' Pond said.

'It does? Would you care to explain how?' John asked, checking skyward again, wishing he had turned on his phone so he could send the clip home to someone on the outside. Someone who could confirm it was his idea of what stood for normal and not theirs that was correct; that such conversations he became regularly embroiled in were surreal. But didn't regularity define normality? He had spent over twenty years telling himself Liverpool's lack of a league title was an anomaly. Wasn't it time to face the facts as they were presented? In this establishment there was an informant and enforcer protocol being run. How else had his lack of tie come to light? Had he, therefore, spent the previous four years working somewhere estranged from what constituted as a regular environment of: mistrust, petty squabbles, incompetent management and a labyrinth of bureaucracy? Or had he been transported into a social project that sought to run itself using Karl Marx's *Theory of Alienation*?

John zoned in on the conversation as Pond came to the point of explaining that, if he had all his ties down at the dry cleaners, Shaft would be more than happy to loan him one of his own, three of which she had out on display. Judging by what the Head of Pastoral Learning and Nurturing Care in the Primary Learning Phase now wore, he had come from meagre beginnings. All three were tired, plain and store bought. They belonged to a first year accountant.

'I'm not sure you answered my question. How does this help children learn?' John said, picking up the middle tie by the point and letting it flop back into position.

'Well, if the children were to enter the learning establishment, they would see how smart everyone was and understand what the expectations were, it would assist in the Elevated Learning and Collective Collaboration,' Pond said, the ties still on offer.

'Men wearing ties is a statement of high expectations. So this relates to what? The desire for the children to also become a teacher or attain jobs where people wear ties? I'm still not sure how it would give a better understanding of their times tables or if, for example, a man stood teaching in a pair of jeans, this would affect the outcome of a lesson on commas in a negative manner,' John replied, starting to feel pangs of hunger.

'Jeans? A teacher wearing jeans?' Pond gasped, casting glances over each shoulder as though Welk or Sugarman were about to appear from the æther.

'I think you might have missed the point,' John replied. 'What I was suggesting is that unless you have research that was conducted by the Victorian Education Board, Old Etonians or the executive members of the tie manufacturing industry, I'm not certain you'll find there's any correlation between wearing a tie and raising educational standards. Especially when there is no direct interface between learner and teacher.'

Pond neatly folded and placed the merchandise carefully into the side pocket of her briefcase.

'Am I to believe that you would rather discuss this matter with the elite senior leadership team?'

'Sure, I'd be more than happy to.'

Pond shook her head; 'I'm not sure you understand Jonathon. I am here to tell you that wearing a tie is in the Staff Handbook of Rules, Regulations and Procedures Edition eighty-four, page eight, point three. Unless you're wearing one tomorrow, you will be issued with a formal verbal warning.'

'Well,' John said, stepping past her as he spoke. 'I'm glad we were able to get straight to the point.'

23.

Acquainting himself fully with the staff handbook from cover to cover, and having decided that if Shaft was presently the bar he was going to raise it, John took himself down to the tailors. There he purchased, for less than an average two-piece, two three-piece wool and cashmere suits.

Presently he was walking down the corridor in the crushed blue option, complimented by a claret cravat and pocket square.

He checked his watch as he strode, an antique pocket version he had purchased via the internet through one of the friendlier local hires. As of yet, removing it from his waistcoat to pop open the cover, it hadn't lost any of its novelty.

Turning left he stopped outside the room that had, since his arrival at the establishment, belonged to Operations, only to find it vacant. John stepped inside the room carefully, as if in doing so he might penetrate the cloak of invisibility that had been thrown up to allow these staff to go unnoticed, undisturbed and work in a more efficient manner. The view from inside, however, was the same as that through the window.

'Err,' he began, hearing footsteps behind him. 'Oh,' he added, as a cleaner came to a halt, carrying a duel set of mop and buckets. They stared at him, taking the strain rather than relinquishing the weight. 'Do you know where they've gone?' John asked, pointing to the huge placard that bore the name of Operational Administrators Office for Assistants in the Servicing, Maintenance and Facilitation for Onsite and Travel for Lyonton International.

The cleaner nodded and wagged his finger down the corridor that led to the main reception foyer that ran the length of the front of the building. The gesticulation that followed, as his arm swung from right to left, bobbing rapidly up and down, was reminiscent of a machine gun. John frowned and the cleaner nodded again before smiling a half toothless grin and struggling off to the toilets.

What awaited John in the foyer was not a pile of bodies and bullet riddled walls, but administrative staff lining the length of the corridor. They sat staggered either side as though they were cars allowing others to pass. John stopped at the first desk to read the job title. It was written in pen on the clean side of a piece of scrap paper which had been folded lengthways. The woman smiled at him, her desk balanced on a bracket against the wall having been sawed down the middle. Her chair was plastic, a bucket-seated one from a former Pre-Primary classroom. On her desk she had one pen, one pencil and no paper.

'Do you know where Vicky is, the lady who sorts the buses?' John enquired.

The woman's head moved in a circular yogic motion; 'I do not know where Vicky is. She has left and her job no longer exists,' she answered softly.

'So no one is in charge of organising the buses anymore?' John asked, sighing inwardly. The football tournament his boys were due to attend was in five days on the other side of the city. He had sent emails to both Vicky's Lyonton account and bookingbus@lyonton, but both of them had failed to deliver. The woman raised a finger, head back to its central position, 'But there is a new position with someone tending the buses,' she added.

John was unsure if the verb to tend was suitable for the un-marked mini vans with drivers who, from prior experience, weren't informed of the destination until he stepped aboard. It had been down to his bilingual centre-back to ride shotgun (knees up on the dashboard to accommodate the bucket and cloths it appeared all drivers were legally required to carry) and navigate.

'She is down in the main office,' the woman concluded.

'By "main office" do you mean randomly in the corridor or...'

'No, main office, the one beside Mr Sugarman,' the woman said, her tone slightly exalted when mentioning the head's name.

John thanked her and moved through the foyer as keys were punched with a hypnotic regularity, each of the seats occupied. There was no slouching, no cups on desks and no personalities. It wouldn't have looked out of place on the ground floor of the Tate Modern.

Most of those he passed, John didn't recognise and he was beyond the clichéd stage of claiming they all looked the same. Every one of them, very briefly, without removing their fingers from their keyboards, smiled and curtly bowed.

The blinds of the extensive office Sugarman resided in were semi-drawn. The glimpse John was allocated showed the head teacher at his desk, a refurbished antique as hulking as his own frame. Every item in the room was imposing, over exaggerated, a removal team's nightmare. There might have been areas of the building being neglected by the under-staffed cleaning team, but this was not one.

John continued down a short corridor to the rooms that ran adjacent. One was the boardroom that was forever in a state of red alert with bottled water and cups to the left of each chair and plates of biscuits piled high in prisms.

To the right of it, and directly behind Sugarman's office, was Ursula's. It was half the size and cordoned off into two sections. It was free of art and everything except her desk was made of plastic. There were filing cabinets in all four corners and a humidifier gently exhaling steam. John expected to hear a soft stream of background music, possibly falling rain or chiming bells, but that would have disrupted the conversation the women were having. They paused as John entered, greeting him even more enthusiastically than their understudies from the corridor. The tall, rakish girl, John had seen before. She was the replacement for Kaley. Her lack of frame was such a defining trait it was almost comical. She was Olive Oil, a cartoon character who would be able to hide behind the trunk of a sapling. She stood, whilst her new colleague remained seated. John could have spotted the resemblance even had she not been dressed in the same fashion as her aunt? Elder cousin? Who sat reading her newspaper in the adjacent office. Three-quarters of the frame of Ursula, it wouldn't be long before she caught up with her relative. The way she sat reminded John of a mollusc, the sturdy back of the chair acting as her spine.

'Hello, how can we help you today?' Olive asked, as the mollusc showed him she had undergone recent dental work. Ursula waved at him, twisting her hand at the wrist, pointing to an assortment of confectionery besides the mollusc's laptop. John signalled he was good to go without.

'I was informed that someone in here is now "tending the buses",' he said, as the mollusc began to swivel from side to side.

'That is me,' she said, selecting not two, but three biscuits.

'Right, well I've tried to send two emails today to book a bus for sixteen of us this Saturday, but it said the email is no longer working.'

'That is right,' the mollusc replied, her nodding revealing the distinct line where her make-up ended, two shades lighter than her skin.

'So is there a new email? Can you book me a bus?'

The nodding gradually transformed to a wobbly shake.

'Email?   Yes, schoolwidetravelandtransportationcoordinator@lyonton, but it's my assistant who will book for you.'

'Right,' John said, 'and she is? Did you maybe consider emailing out these changes to everyone?'

The mollusc's expression did not alter.

'Yes, my assistant should have sent an email. I will deal with this.'

'Well, I'm sure this change has only been implemented today, so if you could just inform me of her name and the desk she's at, I'll be sure to go and sort this out.'

'No, no, she will come to you. Please sit,' the mollusc said, extending her arms until they were at full stretch over her keyboard.

'It's really no trouble for me to...' Deaf ears. John gave up and sat, able to see into the corridor from where, in less than thirty seconds, a woman came scampering. He stood to intercept her but her reprimand had begun as soon as they had heard her footsteps. From over her newspaper Ursula peered, focussing on the reaction of the assistant, satisfied one way or another before the grilling had reached its conclusion.

'Listen, I've a meeting that I really can't be late to, so can I quickly explain to her what I need?' John asked, interrupting the curt, snapped remarks and bowing.

'No need, you leave the request with me and I will fully explain,' the mollusc said. 'You remember my email? Yes? Here, take a business card,' she added, popping open a brand new pack.

'Bone,' she said, tapping her name on the card.

'I guess that makes sense,' John replied, wishing them all a good day before rushing to the stairs with less than two minutes to spare.

When he arrived, the agenda was already written on the board and everyone was sat facing it. John shuffled in beside Carl, who having looked him up and down, indicated that he should take a look at Shaft, Craft and Latte, the three of whom were also wearing cravats and pocket squares.

'Side has been chosen has it?' Carl whispered.

'It was supposed to be a statement.'

'It is. It says "I received the memo because I'm with them".'

'It was supposed to be hyperbole. Look, I've even got a pocket watch,' John said, at precisely the exact moment Shaft brought out his.

'Are you sure you wouldn't feel more comfortable sitting beside them?' Carl asked, tie loose, sleeves rolled at the cuffs.

'I knew I should have bought a hat to go with it,' John sighed, leaning forward, with his elbows on his knees as Welk and Pond entered. The pair of them were holding carry-on luggage.

'Good afternoon everyone,' Welk announced, shoving her bag on top of Pond's, forcing the Deputy Assistant Head of Formal Academic Learning Within Curriculum Hours to walk blindly until Shaft rose to help her. 'This meeting is going to be relatively quick because, as you remember, myself, Miss Pond and our new head of Afternoon Early Years and Foundation Overseer of Development Leading into the Primary Phase, Ms Brewer, are travelling for the week to take a look at nursery schools in the 13th Province.'

'Remember?'

'Definitely didn't receive the memo about that.'

'I'd like to see the minutes.'

Welk had her hands on her hips and was staring their way. 'Yes.'

'Just clarifying it geographically,' John replied, trying to figure out why they were journeying four hours to somewhere that had no relation to the school. There was another Lyonton in Province 1 and he had heard rumours they were applying for a location in the 10th Province, but as far as he was aware, the 13th Province wasn't the epicentre of forward thinking Early Years learning. There was a rare bird sanctuary and some famous statues, but that was about it.

'First on the agenda we wanted to discuss and think about what we are doing to celebrate and praise the success of the children.' Even up to a couple of weeks ago she would have paused at this juncture to give time for reflection on the question, but as it had reached the stage where everyone abstained from doing anything other than staring intently in the speaker's direction so they couldn't be accused of unprofessional conduct, she barely paused to breath.

'Talking only lands you in trouble,' Jenny had recently said at lunch. 'It didn't used to be like this, but a vocal breath is a wasted breath.'

'Currently, as you are aware, we are sending certificates from just class teachers. One special award per class per week for the individual who has impressed more than others. We were thinking though that it might be nice for the children if they received special awards on a more frequent basis from the ASLTT. Kate has created a pro forma so all you have to do is send the email of the child to Kate, with the name of the relevant staff member (Pond Maths, Shaft Art, Craft English, Latte Topic and Myself General Excellence) attached. Good? Well Trevor will email the document we created about this. It fits in excellently with our dedication to Kindness and Life Long Learning Love.'

'Do you think she means Elevated Learning and Collective Collaboration?'

'They don't sound particularly alike.'

Welk had raised her voice, though most of the queries were mouthed.

'Next on the list, a message from Margaret Gillies. She wanted to explain this herself, but unfortunately she was called to an Operational Summit Meeting. What she wants me to remind you is that the budget is increasingly thin. Please make sure you unplug your laptops when you are not using them and be aware that we are in the process of installing a whole new light system that will be sound sensitive. Is that it?'

Shaft very subtly brushed his cravat.

'Ah yes. Finally then, Mr Sugarman has noticed that a lot of staff are...' John was sat waiting for eye contact as he polished his watch with the pocket square. It was enough for Welk to lose her rhythm and carefully take a calculated look around the room. '..a lot of staff are...basically our standard of dress is not up to standard and rather than put something in the staff handbook that may be misinterpreted, there will now be photographs of "Suitable Shaft".'

'I'm going to have to put on a few kilos,' Carl muttered.

'I'm buying stocks in hair gel,' John said, running his hand through his hair, the pair ready for Welk's enquiry and their response beating her question.

'Do we have to wear the same colour as well? Is it a uniform?'

'Not exactly a uniform, no. Shoes should be black or brown.'

'So we can choose our own colour?'

'Well, within reason,' Welk began, checking her watch again. 'As long as it's not garish.'

'Right,' John said. 'And so will there be a swatch sample by the photograph? I assume there will be an equal right's policy at least with aspect to the colour?' he added, Pond back to being a pair of feet with two bags.

'I suspect, I mean, I guess we will take another week or so to finalise the details.'

'So once you've returned from your trip?'

'Ah-ha, hmmm. Yes, maybe. Why don't we discuss it in our meeting next week?'

'So is this new policy live or is it still under evaluation?' John asked, wishing he had bought a monocle.

'Still under evaluation I think,' Welk replied, nodding, heading towards the exit. 'If you have any further questions please do ask Mr Shaft. I'll be on email. Until next week then,' she added, clapping her hands sharply once she was out of the door, her heels quickly clattering in time with Pond's.

'So,' Shaft said, leaning forward, the sleeves of his jacket stretched taut. 'As you can see we've opted for the traditional three-piece. This one is wool, but there are a variety of fabrics available in Johnny D's. It's just around the corner from the big KFC and The City Shopping Mall. I brought a few business cards back with me and if you tell them you're a friend of Shaftey's you'll grab a ten percent discount. They also do alterations for free, say if you've been regularly getting down to the gym for the past couple of months. As far as I'm aware they do nice dresses too, so yeah, well worth getting yourself down there. Any questions?'

Everyone was already on their feet.

24.

'It's true.'

'No! Really?'

'Yeah, I saw some pictures the other day. One of the girls in the office showed me. Eastlife.'

'Better than Westdeath, I guess,' John replied, straightening the feathers of the shuttlecock.

'Made quite a bit of money from it apparently. They played in front of five thousand people, used to do tours of primary schools and old people's homes. He was supposed to be the slightly chubby blonde one. Shane? Wayne? Shaun?'

'I thought they were all slightly chubby and blonde, but maybe that's another boy band I'm thinking of,' John said, easily able to envisage Shaft sat at a stool, microphone in hand with a smile to put the Cheshire Cat to shame.

'I used to go to a gig at least once a month when I was back home, not boy band ones though.'

'Sounds like you're protesting too much,' Ron interrupted, unleashing a smash and then windmilling his arm as though there was more power stored in the joints.

'It's a shame there's nothing on around here like that. Somewhere you can don your grubby Converse, ripped jeans and be handed your drink in a plastic glass,' John said wistfully, ready to start.

'Can't say that I've ever owned a pair of Converse,' Ron stated, stretching his arms one at a time across his chest before raising his headband a fraction. 'And the last concert I went to wasn't my idea. Bon Jovi at Twickenham Stadium,' he continued, signalling he desired an extra couple of minutes warm-up. 'Ended up dancing on stage with him. The guy must have the largest mouth-to-head ratio in the world. Seriously, up close it looks like it could be manufactured, like he was the prototype of the Bratz Doll before they decided to go with over exaggerated eyes instead. He did *Shot Through The Heart* whilst we were up, but I'd say half his set were covers.'

'You sucked someone off for VIP tickets?'

'I didn't, but my girlfriend at the time might have done. She claimed she helped out a couple of roadies who were lost on the subway head in the right direction. Sounds even more dubious now I'm re-telling it. They told her she was welcome to bring a friend. I'd have specified gender, but anyhow.

'The thing I remember most is standing on the field post show, surrounded by these people in mourning that they weren't going to see him again for four or five years. They had to have been platinum members of his fan club. There were five or six of them in t-shirts from earlier tours, mid-thirties, embracing each other with simultaneous tears of joy and despair. It was evangelical.'

'You do wonder how people can grow so attached,' John remarked, ready to serve, as Ron prolonged the start by taking a drink.

'No, I understand attachment: sports team, religion, musician, actor, nature, a country, everyone has something they hold dear to the extent that it seems illogical to others.'

'Hats for example?'

Ron chortled: 'If you will. Yet would I bemoan the loss of a Gap cap? Do you expect to find me a broken man, destroyed by the fact I've lost a product I could find in another store in nearly any city? This isn't Bowie, Prince or Michael Jackson we're dealing with. It isn't an individual who has delivered a set of outstanding, cutting-edge hits. It is a man who has performed karaoke. They'd do fine sitting around in their living room with a DVD of the event. A copy of a copy.'

'Probably best you didn't buy the ticket,' John said, waiting for Ron to signal he was ready to begin.

'I did say to Larissa on the train as we returned home I thought it was strange he hadn't played his theme from *Robin Hood*. It wasn't until the next day at work someone informed me that was Bryan Adams.' He hummed as he set himself, both arms raised in the manner of a man ready to hand himself over to the authorities.

'You do know you're humming Meatloaf's *I Would Do Anything For Love*?'

'Yep.'
'Right, just checking.'

25.

'Do you know what frustrates me most about virtual learning?' Catrina said, perched on the edge of the sofa. A cashmere blanket the colour of an industrial sky was all she wore. 'It's the fact that on a weekend, at ten in the evening, when you've finally retired to bed, one of them is writing an email under the assumption you are in fact a robot-programmed to revolve your life around their needs.

'When I was ten, I'd have been in bed with the lights out a long time ago and if they are on the internet at that time, why would you be asking if you should do both sides of the sheet when you've everything else in the world at your fingertips? Shouldn't they be watching or listening to something they shouldn't be? That's what I was doing when my parents allowed me to have a TV in my room. Isn't that the point of growing up, discovering what was once hidden?

'They're a bunch of nerds that's for sure. I think I learn as much from them as they do from me. During our Great Fire of London topic, one of them sent me a link about Hangzhou. Not only was it one of China's seven ancient capitals, most of the city went up in flames on six separate occasions in the space of a hundred and fifty years prior to the Mongol invasion. Apparently they developed a fantastic firefighting plan, yet kept erecting ramshackle wooden dwellings. There were 10,000 houses lost in the first fire and 30,000 a hundred years later. It made them sound like moths.'

John presented her with a hot chocolate. It was the third time this week she had come round. They had ordered a take away and fucked on the kitchen table. Then they sat in their underwear or less working, watching a DVD, discussing everything as though there would never be a time when they'd be left searching for something to say.

'I prefer it when you set the task and receive an email five minutes later from someone telling you they don't understand. You explain it slightly differently and get told another five minutes later by someone else they still don't understand. You're practically doing the task on their behalves and then, with ten minutes of the lesson to go, have someone appear to tell you their internet connection's been down and they're not sure what to do.'

'I don't geddit.'

'It's impossible to tell if they're making punctuation and spelling mistakes or if they're intentionally using text speak.'

Catrina closed her laptop and pushed it to the side.

'Enough of that for the evening,' she concluded, sipping her drink, commending him on the taste as if he did more than drop in the powder and stir. 'Why don't we play a round of trivia?' she added, letting the blanket fall as she rose to grab two cards from the deck next to the TV. Their play had been inspired by one of John's trips to Serge's to watch football. The PE teacher had done away with the *Trivia Pursuit* board and simply went down the card with the winner being the first to answer ten correct questions.

'Usual rules?' Catrina asked, using John's thighs as a foot rest, reclining against the edge of the sofa with her legs creating a rhombus.

'We're going to have to change them slightly.'

'You never know, I might not get one wrong,' she replied, her forearms covering her nipples. She squeezed down gently so her breasts spilled out at the sides, the colour of fresh dough.

'With your previous record I don't think I can take that chance,'

She dug her heels into his thighs.

'So what do you suggest?'

'For every question wrong, you have to insert a finger.'

'And what about if I answer correctly?'

'You take one out and place it in my mouth.'

'But what about you, do the same rules apply?'

'It's only fair that they do,' John replied, exposing himself, ready to do away with the cards, but Catrina halted him, her soles pressed against his chest.

'Which island's main two ethnic groups are the Tamils and Sinhalese?'

'Sri Lanka.'

'Now it's my turn.'

'Which is the largest company in Switzerland?'

Catrina bent her knees, bringing him closer. Her arms fell by her side. Her right hand rested on the lower section of her stomach. John checked the answer.

'I'm going to say Lindt.'

John shook his head.

'Swatch?'

'Do those count as two incorrect answers? It's Nestle.'

'And there I was ready to guess again,' Catrina purred, her ring finger joining her index and middle as she lowered her right foot to the ground. 'You know in the early days of Hollywood when they had to keep one foot on the ground when they were in bed together? Why didn't they get creative?'

John reached for his phone.

'I think that would be for the best.'

Half an hour later with their drinks having gone tepid, John was at the stove again, whilst Catrina re-watched the final minute of action.

'What were you thinking about?'

John stirred the powder, little brown nuggets forming as it clumped together.

'I was picturing how it was going to end. What it would look like as a video.'

'The lighting could be better.'

'I'm considering investing in a tripod.'

'What do you usually think about?'

'I don't know, it depends.'

'On who you're with.'

'There's so many parameters that can affect it. Sometimes you don't even need to think. Other times it has to be specifics. Most of the time it's a montage reel.'

John paused to taste test. The lowest he could turn the gas wasn't low enough, so the pan balanced at an angle.

'When I masturbate it's always a viable scenario. A glimpse of a desired situation no matter how impractical the consequences of the action would be. Maybe it's because it began pre-sex, when sex itself was the fantasy. I can remember it being this obsession. Reading about it, watching it, needing it. I think when I lost my virginity I shoved it in all her holes for fifteen seconds at a time and then came in her mouth. She'd told me how experienced she was prior. How she'd blown people and wanked them off, but now I think that was bullshit.'

'Forty-five seconds?'

'It might have been less. I remember the second time I came really early but I carried on going because I was aware this woman knew what she was doing and would make a judgement. I kept pumping away until her moaning started to fade. What about you?'

'You mean what's the fastest I've cum or the quickest I've had someone cum? I want to say made, but I suspect I could have been a doll,' Catrina said, signalling she wanted to retire to the bedroom. 'It started when we were standing against the bed,' she continued, holding John by the hips to re-enact it, 'and the force of the opening thrust had me falling back to the bed. When he moaned I thought he'd snubbed his toe, but no it was over before I was on my back. He tried to tell me it was because I was so beautiful, then later it was due to a hyper-sensitive bell end. Whatever it was, he needed to seek medical guidance about it.'

'A single thrust,' John smiled, imagining the awkward silence, the cruel comedy, the audience awkwardly cringing.

'If you could change anything about me, what would it be?'

He liked the way she fit beside him on the bed, like they were a combined salt and pepper pot.

'I can remember when I was younger and my parents decided we were going to be vegetarian. It lasted for four years and in that time they brought me up on Linda McCartney products: pies, pasties, sausage rolls all filled with soy or Quorn. I thought they were brilliant because I had nothing to judge them by. After a year or so the packaging suddenly announced everything was made with an "improved recipe and improved taste". After three mouthfuls I felt cheated.'

'So you're saying that I'm perfect or that I look like a pie?'

'I'm saying I don't want you to change and you're all that stands between me and kwashiorkor.'

26.

As it was his mum's sixtieth birthday on the twenty-first of December, John had booked a flight home for the Christmas holiday before he'd even left for Lyonton. The rest of his friends: Serge, Carl, Ron, Fergie and Catrina had decided to make the most of their new exotic home to book shorter, cheaper hops to locations around the Asian Pacific. Each of them updated him with random photographs on beaches or bars, in skimpy outfits or none at all.

"Warm Shower" was one tag. "What could I wear with these shoes?" another.

John text Catrina every morning and evening and when he thought about the prospect of returning after the break, she was the only lure. Aside from the promise of her, he considered going AWOL frequently. When friends asked what it was like teaching and living abroad he responded by announcing "the money's great". He would acclaim the city for its close proximity to other enticing sites that glistened in glossy magazines, sites he would be visiting in the half-term and Easter breaks.

Since it was also their holiday season, however, he bypassed more friends than he saw. They derided his timing. They were too busy packing or making trips to see relatives. One pointed out they had caught connections in the same airport an hour apart. So aside from watching football at a regular time and visiting the gym when it wasn't closed for public holidays, John shopped in the pre-sales, sales and post-sales until his suitcase could only be closed by sitting astride of it. His mum entered his room as he was reading a graphic novel. She hadn't taken out the earrings he'd bought her since opening the delicate box they came in.

'I've brought you a turkey sandwich,' she announced, shooing his feet so she could occupy the end of the bed. 'And the quiz is on in twenty minutes,' she added, her attempt to move his suitcase with a nudge of her foot futile. She bent to try and lift it but that was no good either.

'You know they won't allow a bag over thirty-two kilos?'

'It's thirty-one point seven,' Johnathon replied, three pages shy of the end of the chapter.

'I suppose you become an expert with the weight when you're a frequent flyer. Keeps you a little younger too, although I wonder if jet lag doesn't offset that? I mean you feel like you've aged when you're tired and certainly it presents that way in terms of appearance.'

'I hadn't give it any consideration,' John said, giving up on the book.

'You know darling, your dad and I have been attempting to work out just how you're feeling about your job and living overseas. Was it the right decision do you think?'

John hummed as he slowly bobbed his head, weighing up the question. Life was more than work, but work was what he spent a third of his day doing, so if he were to create a sum to work out if the answer drew a positive or negative, it might err either way.

'It's hard to tell at the moment. I mean no matter what job you're in you're always going to have complaints. There are always areas for improvement which will never be addressed because you're so far down the ladder (or high up on some misplaced tree branch). You realise it's easier to say nothing at all and simply churn through the hours until you can go and have fun in whatever slender allocated time of the day you have left, whilst counting down the weeks, days and finally hours before your holidays.'

'Come now, that's not how you felt about school here though darling. You always said you liked being a teacher,' his mum said, taking a bite of the sandwich herself before rising to set a couple of books on the shelf straight.

'I did. I do. I don't quite know. The children seem to be engaged. They send me through pictures they've drawn. I'm usually Asian in them, but really tall and I wear glasses and have these black school shoes on. It's nice to know that they care and I'm important enough that they're taking their time to design something for me, but it's everything else that corrodes the soul, drains my energy, time and resources.'

'Well there's nothing forcing you to stay there for the whole contract. Why don't you leave in July?'

'Because there's a ten percent bonus, because I want a decent reference, because I reckon if I just hang on in there then there's going to be an opportunity on the ladder for me. The person who hired me sent an email yesterday about a meeting on the fifth.'

'But you don't leave here until the sixth.'

'Yes, I think she meant the fifteenth. To be honest she spelt her job title incorrectly so maybe it was her PA who sent it out, but it said it was about my long term future.'

'That's nice. That sounds very positive and remember the name Lyonton still resonates.'

'Well, less than it did four months ago, but yes, it's still impressive to the ears of those not in the know.'

27.

'This does not mean we are being forced outside of the Lyonton family, this means we, as an establishment, are being allowed to compete on our own terms alongside it.' Sugarman changed the slide with his pen to bring up a flow chart so convoluted it made Welk's decision tree look like a minimalist masterpiece. Arrows were overlaid with arrows. When anything was this complex, legitimacy had to be questioned. 'Firstly, let me assure you that what you see here in transparent terms, legitimises the whole process we have been, and are continuing, to go through.'

Sugarman had occupied his podium for the past hour and a half. Most of it had been a drudgery of accountancy, maintenance costs and minutes from board meetings that had nullified everyone to the point where this significant news was met by only a few stirs and scratches of the head.

The premise of the whole school staff meeting, presented boldly in capital letters on the opening slide, had been *Lyonton International; Looking to the Future and Beyond*. When John had entered he had thought it was a light-hearted Hollywood pun meant to entice a small chuckle.

'Are you hearing this?' he asked Serge, who was bent over his phone, chewing at the skin on his fingers.

'I'm online searching for new jobs, have been since we broke for Christmas. There's been so many nails over the past eighteen months it's hard to see the coffin.'

'Did you know this was happening?'

'Heard a rumour. The real Lyonton sent over some of their key board members and they weren't impressed by the image we were presenting. They claimed it was having a negative effect on the brand. Sugarman took it to mean they wanted their cut increasing but that wasn't the case. We weren't "complementing the ethos and mentality steeped in the Lyonton tradition" therefore we will henceforth be known as Lyonton International Pristini until all the litigation is finished.'

'Is that Latin?'

'Yep, for former. It adds another level of pretension that makes us sound even more important than the real deal. For those parents who don't bother to check its meaning it's a winner. Plus most people assume it means pristine.'

'Is this happening with the other schools across the Lyonton franchise?' John asked, as Sugarman unveiled the new logo, identical except with *Pristini* a line and a half underneath and two font sizes smaller.

'No, the others are appropriately representing the foundations of the grand establishment. However, they should keep a breakaway in mind for a short term economic boost because our enrolment is up eighteen percent from this same period last year.'

To John's right, one of the Post-Primary science teachers who had been with the school since its foundation, slowly straightened and blinked repeatedly. This latest development was likely to have as much effect on him as anything else in the previous six years. He was one of those impervious, superficially at least, to the internal and external mandates that were regularly and sporadically passed. John wanted to inquire what motivated him. He understood that for some it was the convenience of staying - the idea of relocating, re-writing a CV, applying, interviewing, rejection, repeating, packing up and stepping into the unknown once again was daunting. Had he run away from his life at home? Was he escaping painful memories like Carl had alluded to? Maybe he was a government mole? John had heard there were local hires who had links to higher authorities. They were untouchable and he should be weary of how he spoke in their vicinity. Perhaps the secret service had decided to plant someone outside of their normal roster.

'Have you applied for anything?'

'Found a Head of PE job in Tehran. It's a sideways step but at this stage I'd happily accept a single crazed ayatollah than a pack of soulless puppeteers. I'll give you an example of my most recent dealings with the extended hierarchy of this place, the three-inch iron nail if you will. Sports Day is under my jurisdiction. It's on the final Friday of April unless it coincides with a holiday, but it's always in the calendar a year in advance.'

'Is this the same master calendar I was introduced to at the start of the year that's now on version twenty-one?'

'We're up to twenty-four now. Last year we made it to thirty-three so I think they're on course to beat it. Anyway, there I am thinking I'll make sure all the equipment is accounted for and working, as it can be time consuming ordering certain items. I find we're two parachutes short. I place an order request only to be told by finance it's been rejected because my "ring-fenced" budget has been spent for the year. So I go and see HOAASTSD who knows nothing of the siphoning of cash, but would like a copy of the scheduled events.

'Then I'm called into a meeting by Ryan whose new title, I'm informed as I sit across from her, is Head of Pastoral Projects Within The Post-Primary Timetable. Since Sport's Day is now technically under her jurisdiction, she wants it to be more inclusive. I tell her I'll see what I can do.

'Next day Head of Post-Post...The Sixth Form, wants to meet due to the fact he's scheduled exams on that day and now there's a clash. I try to point out that of course there's a clash as he's arranged them on Sport's Day. Off I go to the Big Cheese himself for some kind of clarity, but as soon as I've introduced my topic he tells me that I'm best to meet with the Head of Post-Primary first. She explains that she can't see any reason why the exams and Sports Day can't work around each other, but that it would be best to check with the Chief of Facilities on Campus Including The External Gate before I proceed any further. In order to run an event, I have to gain stamped approval which I can then scan into a booking form to send her. You still with me?' John nodded slowly. 'Good. So I walk in to Facilities to find Margaret Gillies in the main chair.'

'Margaret Gillies? The Margaret Gillies? The one in charge of recruitment and something else,' John said, as Sugarman touched on the legalities of their situation and the processes.

It brought to mind an anecdote John had overheard a member of the Post-Primary staff delivering. He had recently arrived from Moscow and was explaining about a school that had failed to keep up with its official visa process. It had been forced to shut overnight with all of its staff thrown onto the next available flight to Finland with only hand luggage. When they reached Helsinki they were all informed they faced a six-year ban on re-entering Russia and their assets in the country were being frozen.

'Margaret Gillies is a story for another time. She's had more rolls than Jack, Jill and everyone who's ever visited Cooper's Hill. The legend, and that's all we have to go by, is that when she was interim head teacher during a four-month reign three years ago, she drew up her own contract that stated she could never be in a position below that from which she had previously been. Technically this means her job of ticking sheets to allocate rooms and areas on the compound usurps the Deputy Head. She's like some indestructible chess piece.'

'She sent me an email during the holiday asking me to attend a meeting before we were due back. She spelt her title incorrectly and I had assumed it was the mistake of a local hire,' John said, as the meeting encroached upon its second hour.

'What do we know about assumptions? Last year a member that was leaving created a Buzzfeed entitled; *Twenty times you read and re-read a Margaret Gillies email and still couldn't understand it*. The reason it was such an acclaimed success was because they were forced to pare it down. It was like Prince with *Purple Rain*, five options for each available slot. But alas, I regress. I'm standing there in front of Margaret talking about ratifying an event that was sanctioned over a year ago when she suddenly interjects and asks me if the Head of PE knows this conversation is taking place.'

'But how did she manage to become interim head?' John asked, unable to believe all he was being told was true. There had to be grains of salt littering each portion of a one sided story. Simon shrugged,

'I'm not entirely sure, but it would make for a cracking Aesop's Fable.' He flicked left on his screen. 'An Athletic Director position in Mosul, don't mind if I do.'

28.

Margaret's previous office had been glass backed. It had been two-thirds the size of Sugarman's and less ornate. That space was now dedicated to a small-scale example of a learning pod for prospective parents and students to experience whilst she had been relocated to the facilities hub. The hub wasn't subterranean, yet those who had created it had done everything to make it appear that way. The note on the door was a laminated piece of card rather than an oversized board attached to the wall. The miniature step, which could have been warping from water damage, had been zealously patched with striped electrical tape raising it another inch.

As he entered, John expected to encounter loose wires and yellows triangles warning him he was dangerously close to death, levers, a loud buzzing and a cylindrical pole grinding slowly on its axis.

'Hello?'

It wasn't quite as derelict. The walls hadn't been painted and it was gratuitously under lit, but aside from that it struck John as more of a research facility than a maintenance room. There was a block of screens showing CCTV footage and panelling that ran the length of the wall with various nodules, dials and joysticks embedded, some of which rhythmically pulsed. On the opposite wall there were laminated procedures struggling for space: flow charts, numbers, bullet points, passport sized photographs of those responsible for enforcing whatever the writing dictated, all of which was bold, underlined and in block capitals. At a glance, John couldn't determine if they ran left to right or from top to bottom.

'Yes?'

Margaret was sat at a workbench loaded with box files, the screen of her laptop penetrating through the gloom.

'I'm here for the meeting,' John announced, noticing two sets of firemen's uniforms hanging high on the panelled wall. Margaret studied him, her pupils on the verge of breaking through her irises and seeping into the sclera.

'You're here to discuss the fitting of the motion sensor lights?'

John shook his head slowly.

'I suppose I must be the other one,' he replied, watching people in black and white move across the large monitors, the time ticking over in the bottom corners.

'You'll have to excuse me while I consult my calendar,' Margaret said, swivelling back to her laptop, jabbing the screen with her finger as she brought up a calendar more densely packed than the procedure wall.

'Ah yes, Johnathon Downton. I called this meeting before my position changed, but we should proceed with it since it is still in my calendar. Please, find a seat,' she said, a scan of the room leaving John remaining where he was.

'Find one from, like outside?'

'Yes, that sounds like a good idea,' Margaret admitted, placing her laptop on her knees so her face was lit and full of concentration. The grey in her hair was more pronounced than when she had stood behind the booth telling him he was what they were looking for.

'So,' she started, with John still heading to the door. 'You managed to win third place in the Under Nineteen football tournament.'

'Well, I'm not sure you can win third. That's where we finished. We should have reached the final. We missed a penalty when we were a goal down and then our keeper committed an error he's probably still struggling to come to terms with,' John said, returning to the spot he had recently vacated.

'In the previous two years we've finished seventh and eighth, so this caught my eye as well as Mr Sugarman's.'

'I'm glad that we've been able to make some progress.'

'The question I now have is how do we ascend to top spot?'

'You mean aside from having the children in for physical PE slots and at least half a pitch to utilise twice a week?'

'That's correct.'

'Well, I mean aside from those, I could have a think. I could put some drills into place, maybe create a programme that could be started with the younger students so by the time they reach the first team there isn't still a need to go over the basics.'

'Excellent! That sounds exactly what we're after. So if you can send me that as soon as you're done, I'll look over it and pass it on to Sugarman,' Margaret said, speaking with the belief her opinion was still valued by the head, despite the fact he had buried her in a bunker without heating and asked her to make sure the toilets were kept clean.

'Right,' John replied, integral coaching drills underpinning stages of development already in mind. The jigsaw pieces of a mission statement were beginning to form. Positive results leading towards a reward. Meritocracy.

Buoyed by the concept of such a scheme, John locked himself away inside his flat with pencil, ruler, paper and laptop and didn't rest until the fifty-page document was complete. He didn't worry too much about the fact he was going to pass the dossier to someone with no knowledge of sport beyond a passing interest in The Olympics and Wimbledon. It was a slide onto the bark of the trunk.

29.

Hunched over his laptop and engaged in a conversation with a pupil from whom he was trying to elicit a reasonable excuse, John was interrupted by Balder, the HOAASTSD. He squeezed inside John's cubicle, his vasectomy inducing shorts level with John's eye line.

'I've just come to let you know I've left your team's sign-up sheets in your pigeon hole,' he announced, giving John a pat on the shoulder as he exited.

'But why not just hand them to me?' John muttered, as his student, with even greater determination and worse grammar than before, attempted to explain the failure to do his maths was because he had lost the sheets.

YOU CANNOT LOSE THEM. THEY ARE ON

THE SERVER. THE LINK DOES NOT EXPIRE. IT IS STILL THERE. LOOK.

John responded, the font size increased to thirty-six.

A string of ellipsis ran across the screen signalling an imminent response, the line falling in waves like a shaken rug.

Ive dun this won

The size of the font a homage perhaps? An assumption of a new standard?

John deleted what he had typed in the aftermath and bashed the lid down. Now he would have to write an email. Then he would have to send it to one of the assistants to translate, forward that to parents and receive an email in reply that would most likely say their son was telling the truth at first (so his assistant would translate for him) and...

He pushed open the staff room door and headed straight for his pigeon hole, sorting what was stored into a relevant pile and what should have been residing in the bin. He was ready to exit with his usual swiftness when he spotted, over at a table in the corner, looking as forlorn as if he had been stood up and lingered until the candle had died out, Carl. His friend raised his head slightly.

'Hey, why so glum?'

'Why so positive?' Carl responded, as John took the chair opposite, the staffroom resembling the admin corridor with miniature tables with a maximum occupancy of two running the length of the far wall.

'Margaret Gillies has asked me to design a football programme for the whole school. Apparently they want to boost results. I put your name down as someone who could help lead it.'

Carl offered half a smile of appreciation.

'Well, I'm in here as part of the improvement plan I have to follow. Welk claimed that my "negative attitude" was due to my "lack of social interaction with the whole faculty" and that from now on I needed to "cheer up" by spending quality time with my colleagues. I tried to tell her I already did that at the lunch table and after school on a Friday playing football, but she claimed the staffroom had been "created specifically to increase positive emotions and mindfulness to emit through the campus". Just take a look around. Oh and who created the word and terminology "mindfulness", the same women who wrote *Eat, Love, Pray*?'

It was a space similar to the gym John visited at home in that no matter what time he turned up, the same people were on the same machines. Here people sat around one of the two circular tables that remained, nursing tepid drinks, shaking and nodding their heads, each taking a turn to concur and entrench whatever view had been raised.

'I don't know, it looks like it usually does to me. I suspect it's what 99.9% of staff rooms look like across the globe. Like hospital rooms,' John remarked, insisting that, with time as it stood, they could go elsewhere.

'What I want to know is how come they always attract the busiest people?' Carl asked, as they made their way up the stairs past sections of the corridor that were now out of commission and cordoned off by a line of PE cones as they underwent a change in lighting.

'It's amazing how quickly they've started on this project,' John said, pointing to a pair of men inserting halogen bars.

'It's their top priority. Sugarman named it number one on his action list. When he wants something doing, it happens instantaneously.'

Ahead of them, coming round the corner, they could hear Welk talking to people and it wasn't Pond or Shaft. John and Carl slowed their pace so as not to merge with them and, hanging back, saw Welk flanked by two men. One of the men was tall, of distinction, possibly an alumni of the real Lyonton itself. The other awkwardly semi-skipped to keep pace, his jacket sleeves a fraction too long, his monk's tonsure fraying at the edges. Welk nodded, facing whichever of the men was talking, her replies a series of *hmms* to show she fully understood.

'An attempt to regain Lyonton's accreditation? I don't recall any minutes surrounding a visit, though I suppose a set of governors could have arrived unannounced.'

'Could it be that we're looking to sell ourselves to a new partner?' Carl pondered, the conversation between the three ahead of them far too hushed for John and Carl to even make out accents clearly.

As it transpired, they weren't made to wait long to discover the identities of the two men. The following morning they were summoned to a meeting by first Shaft, then Pond and finally, to make certain they hadn't missed the previous two messages, Welk herself.

'Good morning everyone and what a fine morning it is. There are two.'

'Three.'

'Three.'

'Four.'

'Four items on our agenda this morning. Mr Shaft, would you like to go first?'

'This week we will be continuing with light maintenance, not light as in the opposite of heavy, but light as in what allows you to see. Please make sure you stay on the other side of the cones that have been placed on the floors. So not on the inside, but the outside, away from the side where the work is taking place. Unless of course that is happening on the outside, but there should be signs explaining this.'

'Excellent Mr Shaft, I have certainly noticed how much dimmer and cosier the corridors have been looking recently,' Welk said, turning to Pond, who sat forward, reading from a small Post-it pad.

'We will be doing levelling on Monday, so remember to bring along six pieces of writing to moderate: high, slightly high, just above average, average, low and below expectations. I'll email you all a reminder about that now and one closer to the time.'

'Inspirational Miss Pond! A really crucial time for us to check the progress and achievements of the children,' Welk said, clapping, as upbeat as anyone had seen her since before the Christmas break.

'Well I start with some very good news. Yesterday we were paid a visit by the new governors who stated that (she withdrew her small, black book) "the primary section continues to improve and develop. The results are positive".' The glances could not be hidden.

'Err,' Jenny started, unable to help herself. 'Isn't that what the Lyonton governors told us last month before severing ties?'

'They said that the time before too,' another voice piped up. 'And the time before that.'

Welk searched the vicinity from which the statement had arisen. She leafed carefully through the black book, which now John thought about it, was surprisingly only half full.

'No. There are similarities, but no. And please remember, as Mr Sugarman has stated on numerous occasions, ties were never severed, they were loosened slightly and we chose to wriggle free. The important message that you should be taking from me, the crux that will be highlighted in the minutes, is that it is obvious to any governor who sets foot in our section of the building that the ASLTT are developing everything; you, the pupils, the motivation to learn, the path of Kindness and Life Long Learning Love, in a constant upward trajectory.'

'To where?' Jenny muttered, under her breath, making John take a mental note to lunch with her next week to ascertain exactly what was happening.

'And finally, the other day, Mr Sugarman and I were admiring The Decision Tree. We both suddenly realised that to make the tree expand and help the leaves become ever more vibrant, we must have new, longer roots. So we agreed to create a new position of Deputy Leader

Overseeing Both Pastoral and Academic Responsibilities Within The Primary Phase.'

Carl raised his hand, another of his improvement actions to "be more involved within staff meetings", a line that John expected to soon be implemented in everyone's contracts.

'Will this be a position directly beneath yours?' he asked, his interest in the answer revealed in the immediate cessation of eye contact.

'Yes, that is the case. Although all roots have a lateral importance.'

'And will this position be filled internally?' Jenny inquired, the silence emitting from Pond's keyboard suggesting this new role was news to everyone. Shaft collected his papers from the floor, crossed his legs one way and then the other.

'No, no one was considered internally. It was decided that we had to search for a root that has long been underground, established already in such a sturdy position if you will.'

'And they're going to be starting when?' blurted Pond, her face pallid.

'You may have seen Mr Gunt walking with me the other day. He shall be with us fully before the Easter break. We will be holding an event to welcome him in the next few weeks. Have a good Friday everyone, you deserve it!'

30.

As they hadn't exchanged any wrapped gifts since the Christmas period, Catrina insisted they abscond into town after work and dine at a teppanyaki restaurant she claimed to have discovered by chance. She wore a slender black dress which was frilly at the hem. It could have been a ballet costume she'd owned since she was twelve. They spent the taxi ride with their hands attached to one another and exited dishevelled, contemplating immediately paying for a return.

Perhaps for the sake of the other customers they were seated in a shadowy corner with a bottle of wine rather than the two glasses they had requested. John suspected that, though he had never fantasised about such a scenario, he would have eventually conjured it. They were squeezed together, a refrigerator conveniently located behind Catrina so no one could tell where his fingers were hiding. She held his left hand with her right as though the fluttering eyelids were due to some awkward arm wrestling competition.

'That's it,' she whimpered, relaxing her pelvic muscles, her thighs releasing the grip on his hand. Before returning it, she sucked on the fingers.

'If I gave you a survey would you be satisfied?'

John nodded, squirming as she rubbed her hands over his crotch.

'Did you miss me?' He continued to move his head in the same manner, the rest of the room becoming a frosted impressionist blur. 'Are you loyal?'

'Err…'

A waitress emerged from the background bringing the scenery to life once again. She laid down a platter of plates, promising to return with another bottle. John pondered the word "loyal". It reminded him of a dog, yet he supposed he had been loyal. Whatever it was they were involved in (and it had never been discussed until now), it had been exclusive. He hadn't considered screwing, dating or sharing a taxi with anyone else. But then if he'd been approached, who knew what action he would have taken. Further explanation wasn't required for the time being, however, as Catrina was released from the taxi ride's spell by the waitress' intervention. She picked up her chopsticks and asked what developments he had heard about his football programme.

The answer was nothing, not even a reply to say his documents had been received. It was a hefty tome though, and after opening it, Gillies had likely been forced to seek clarification regarding certain terminology she was unfamiliar with. He would give her another week to assess it before following it up.

What he had heard, however, from dining at Jenny's table, was that in order to prevent groups gathering during lunch to talk over alternative facts, lunch duties were going to be brought in. These included checking laptops in the Educational Curriculum Transfer Hall in case any immediate correspondence needed to be undertaken during the fifty-minute period in the middle of the day.

'Sounds like the government's reaction to the Second Summer of Love,' Catrina said, re-filling his glass despite him having only taken the most meagre of sips.

'Except in banning random meetings of revellers in fields, they inadvertently created the need for large commercial spaces that could be easily policed as well as taxed. What management should have done was create a rota so one of them was always sitting in the canteen. Instead, it will now be groups of two and three talking together, distortion will happen as things get passed further down the line, and it will become harder to track where the information came from.'

At their table, two plates of sushi, strips of beef and a heap of squid marinated in a light soy sauce were brought before them. This time John spoke with his hand covering whatever he was shovelling into his mouth.

'You know at my old school, an actual school, not an "educational lifestyle facility for future leaders that focusses on Kindness and whatnot" the head and I would sit and chat sometimes. I would go and speak to him about an idea or vice versa and we'd consider the implications both long and short term. Although an idea may seem brilliant, you have to project what effects it will have further down the line. You're never going to be absolutely certain of what can and will happen, sure, but you can speculate likelihoods. Here, however, you have the feeling that when an idea is announced, everybody nods their heads and then they all fail to comprehend why it wasn't a success. Every one of them is in a hurry to trip over the other to showcase their incompetency. And you know what I'm beginning to fear? What if this isn't unusual? What if this is normality and I was lucky before?'

'What, you're not lucky now?' Catrina asked, teasing him with her chopsticks.

'In certain ways I'm very fortunate indeed,' John replied, as another mound of food was delivered to their table. Feeling like this latest platter would satisfy his savoury side, John turned to request a dessert menu and noticed a familiar face tucked away at the edge of one of the long teppanyaki tables. Slumped, dejected and staring questionably, almost argumentatively at his reflection, was Trevor Shaft.

'It's Shaftey,' John pointed out.

'Indeed it is,' Catrina replied, showing greater interest in the fried rice.

'I'm going to go over and say hi,' John said, teetering between the tables, apologising as he ricocheted off occupied chairs.

'Shaftey! How's it going?' he asked, far more jovially than he had intended. With the chair beside his line manager vacant, John dumped himself in it and began to commend the cuisine as though it were a haunt he frequented.

Shaft offered him a beer, apparently attempting to drink half a dozen by the time the meal was over. John acquiesced, stating he was fit to burst. When he had spotted him originally, John had expected to find a lovely leaning on his arm. Someone slender, dark possibly, a local wearing even less than Catrina. However, the seat held no warmth and there were no signs: scarves, handbags, jackets that showed someone would be returning.

'Hung out to dry,' Shaft mumbled, addressing his moping reflection. 'Hung out to dry for what? Wanting better for the children. I wasn't always like this you know.'

John nodded and gave a gentle pat on Shaft's shoulder.

'I used to be the most popular teacher in school back home. "The Shaft!" is what kids and parents called me. I was like a superhero. Fun. Exhilarating. Learning; they couldn't get enough of it. I was here, there, everywhere. Planning events, dressing up, acting, singing, dancing. You know I even had a call to go on *Singing Superstars* but I turned it down because I loved my job, well, I wasn't going to be given the time off. And look at me now.'

He pulled at the lapel of his jacket, watching himself do it. The silk inner lining was slightly visible. The colour matched his tie and pocket square.

'I'm beginning to look like him,' he added, exaggerating his size by puffing his cheeks and raising his shoulders. 'You know what he said to me in my second week? "You want to go far here, nod your head and follow your leader". And so that's what I did. I tongued arse and sure enough I become assistant pastoral and whatever the rest of the bollocks it now is. You know I have to use the front and back of my business card to fit it on,' he continued, fumbling for one, bringing it out between his middle and index fingers with a flick. John accepted it so that Shaft might continue.

'And everything felt good because I had a title and more cash to spend and I could get my hair cut at Tony & Guy every week. But then I used to play tennis and footie too. I had muscle definition. Biceps, triceps, abs, six of them. But they've disappeared quicker than a packet of biscuits in Sugarman's office since I'm in meetings every bloody evening. Do you know we've held meetings about how to improve our meetings? And that she considered changing them to "get togethers" to make them seem "cooler" but didn't in the end because it would have "belittled their significance".'

Shaft sighed heavily and downed another beer, his food barely touched.

'You know in my first year here I dated a new girl every week, sometimes two. Expat, local, tourists. I'd go and stay in a hostel on sporadic weekends. Now, well in the last couple of weeks, I keep having these sex dreams and yet I'm never involved. I'm always a spectator. I'll be sitting there in a three piece drinking a coffee or eating a slice of pizza and they'll be fucking away. Two girls. A girl and a guy. I'm in touching distance but I just sit and watch. It's not like I'm even admiring or cheering them on. I literally don't move until it's all over and then I thank them and exit my flat.'

John used the pause to check his table. Catrina was no longer there and it was being cleared away. He brought out his phone and found two messages from her.

'You know what got me into trouble? I'd been watching what everyone new was doing: you, Carl, Fergie, how you were bringing exciting, innovating learning to your children and I thought this is how it should be. It woke me up, made me want to be a creative force again. A month ago I informed Welk that I'd drawn up a couple of fun events for the forthcoming term. I told her we could inspire the pupils through excitement and enjoyment. Two hours later Sugarman demanded my presence to tell me that we have fun on our three community days throughout the year and that if I think differently maybe I'd best trot off to clown college.'

John nodded, making out he had been paying attention.

'You know there's so many stories I could tell you. Are you sure you don't want a beer? To share a beer?'

John re-read the last message; *I think I'm going to eat my dessert in the back of a taxi.*

'I'd love to,' he said, already standing, 'but I've really got to shoot.'

31.

John suspected Pond might legally qualify as a dwarf if she ever removed her platform heels. Was a dwarf someone under 4'11"? Was there a legal limit or was it some myth he'd been taken in by and never bothered to ascertain the truth of?

Presently she stood in the middle of the room presenting in the style of her superior by reading slides from the interactive board. Beside every teacher, much to the chagrin of those leading the meeting and their conservative photocopying demands, were reams of paper from the latest rounds of writing assessments and the new reading assessments to be implemented in the final term. Pond was extolling the virtues of a new reading scheme, explaining how assessments would be conducted and how the mark scheme worked and the four places the results should be recorded.

John could remember as a boy having a *Facts and Lists* book filled with interesting statistics and tables and how his dad, whenever he read through a list, would explain he had to take the scores of the USSR with a pinch of salt. The foreman, the labourer, the executive, the supervisor, all in agreement that once again it had been a record year for iron production. Beside him Carl had been shaking his head for the past five minutes and now Pond could ignore it no more.

'Is everything okay Mr Caldwell?'

'No, not really,' Carl said, ignoring the fact that Welk, a few feet behind the shoulder of Pond, was suddenly interested, tapping at her pockets. Shaft looked away. 'We did our assessment earlier in the year to set a baseline standard for the children, one which can be measured throughout the year so that we, as teachers, can monitor their progress. However, these new tests you're bringing in do not have any correlation to what we've already done. Aside from the fact they give different levels to what we have been using, they're multiple choice. It's like me looking at where the pupils are in the league at Christmas and then, despite their position in February, celebrating the fact they're still in the cup. Actually let me give another analogy. It's as though I've first marked their performance on the parallel bars and now I want to assess against that but I'm going to watch their pummel horse routine. Plus, it doesn't give the parents a chance to expand on the reasoning behind their answers.'

'I'm sorry, parents?' Pond asked, checking over her shoulder for a signal as how best to proceed. John leaned forward.

'Football programme,' he muttered with his elbows on his knees, rocking back and forth in the manner of a man about to be restrained.

'Let's look at the facts, shall we,' Carl replied, patting his pile of paper. 'Surely I'm not the only one who finds that on a day to day basis work is littered with mistakes and often turned in half finished. Yet as soon as we explain that the work is an assessment piece they all transform into Shakespeare.'

There were nods from around the room.

'Research has suggested that children, when given a task, and having had a set of expectations placed upon them, raise their standards accordingly by taking into consideration their prior learning. Our children make extremely rapid progress once they are under our tutelage and our results showcase that. It is all to do with our Kindness and Life Long Learning Love.'

'Oh, I can clearly see just how outstanding the progress has been. I'd like to read an extract from Jina who has previously, on more than one occasion, failed to spell her name properly.

'"*Why there is no remedy; it is the curse of service. Preferment goes by letter and affection and not by old gradation, where each second stood heir to the first.*"'

John looked around the room.

'Very good, some wonderful vocabulary there.'

'I should hope so. It's act one, scene one from *Othello*,' Carl replied.

The room suddenly burst into spontaneous laughter as Pond backed away a little. She checked with Shaft and Welk, neither of whom moved alongside her nor beckoned her to take a seat. 'Now I'm not saying that everyone in the Primary section is cheating, but I'm going to go ahead and put my neck on the line here and pick a piece at random. Let's see.'

He was up on his feet, hands out, sheets being passed his way as he waltzed around the room like the Pied Piper. He gave them a shuffle, closed his eyes and fanned them out in front of Fergie who was sitting cross-legged, a wry smile letting him know she was enamoured by the spectacle.

John kept glancing towards the door expecting bouncers or a man with a Taser, but Carl continued, removing his tie as he took centre stage.

'Here is Kolin. I'm sure some of you will know Kolin and be well aware of what he can already produce, but let's take a snapshot of his current ability.

'"*A minute's bustle, a banging of the coach doors, a swaying of the vehicle to one side, as the heavy coachman, and still heavier guard, climbed into their seats; a cry of all right, a few notes from the horn...*"'

'Ladies and Gentlemen, Kolin shouldn't be at the school formerly known as Lyonton International, he should be given a professorship at Oxford, or Yale perhaps. I mean the way the vehicle sways under the weight of the patrons, the forethought, the technique. I fair he could teach us a couple of things.'

'It's *Nicholas Nickleby*,' Latte said flatly. 'I've just been reading it, wouldn't have known otherwise,' he added, his focus his shoes and his chair tilted at fifteen degrees.

'What the Dickens?!' Carl responded, celebrating by spreading his arms wide and shaking his jazz hands. It was a moment that would be passed down in exulted whispers for years to come.

It would later transpire that he had already packed his bags and had been staying in a hotel near the airport for the previous two nights. He forwarded John his home address in an email with details of where he was heading next. He also sent an email from Sugarman two weeks after he had departed explaining that, due to the fact he had failed to appear at seven previous disciplinary meetings he was being suspended with pay. As that didn't turn out to be a typing error, the day after he had cleared his account, Carl sent an email to all staff from a tropical beach. Two hours later it had been deleted from the server alongside every other email in every Lyonton International account.

32.

For those who remained in the educational facility formerly known as Lyonton, the repercussions in the immediate aftermath started positively. All meetings were cancelled for a week and the daily email count dropped to single digits.

Out on the AstroTurf, where the population of those doing sporting activities had multiplied to the extent it looked like a large scale game of sardines, Serge was prophesying the downward trajectory that was to come.

'I heard they've been talking about curfews. That they'll demand your phone codes. Wages are going to be paid in two instalments; on the fifteenth and at the end of the month.'

Indeed, when John returned to the building to collect his laptop that evening, the attempts to reaffirm order had started to filter down. Mr Gunt's arrival would only be welcomed by a delegation of the ASLTT. His first introduction to "other staff" would be through formal introductions during Learning Walks he would be completing with Mrs Welk. Considering John was still awaiting his observation four months after it had been threatened, he paid the message little heed.

However, two days later, halfway through period three, as he sat scrolling through a website in search of a complimentary resource for the current rainforest topic, in popped Welk and Gunt. They craned their necks around the wall of the booth, their bodies squashed together. Although Welk, in her heels, was at least a foot taller than the new Deputy Assistant Vice Principal Manager of the Primary Section of the School Formerly Known as Lyonton International, the way she stooped made them appear a single entity, like some unfortunate Siamese doctors had refused to receive.

John rose, blocking any entry. Gunt was the man he and Carl had witnessed walking the corridor with Welk, the one with the awkward gait. From the front he appeared friendlier. His goatee had been precisely shaped, but the hair within the boundaries of it was as wild as the tufts that remained around the outer edge of his scalp.

'You must be Mr Gunt,' John said, offering his hand, the deputy's affable handshake and smile in juxtaposition to Welk's scowl. Her eyes darted around his workspace as if following a fly.

'And you're...' he looked down at his clipboard, 'Fergie?'

'No, John or Mr Downton,' John replied, guessing Gunt could have assumed his parents were big Manchester United fans.

'And shouldn't you be at your computer teaching science now?' Welk questioned, pen hovering over her clipboard.

'Fergie might, but I have a free. They're doing art this period and next. I'm in the process of collecting resources for my lesson on rainforests after lunch though if you wish to watch,' John said, hands on his keyboard to resuscitate his monitor.

'I think we have seen enough. I will have Kate email you an appointment time for you to come and be given your feedback,' Welk stated, both her and Gunt waiting for the other to move. Then they both went at the same time. The stop motion movements repeated so their exit was almost as lengthily as the observation itself.

'But what can you achieve in a one-minute observation?' John asked, walking alongside Ron to the badminton court.

'See if you're actually at your desk, spot that your computer's on.'

'It's a bit of a short tick list. I was expecting them to say they'd come back later when my lesson was actually on, but everyone else told me they had only received a minute too. You sit in meetings with those at the top, has there been any justification or rationalisation for it?'

Ron swatted the air.

'My meetings don't involve anything to do with learning. As far as I'm concerned I'm an advertiser first, marketing manager second and show room salesman third. I can tell you one thing though, there's something huge in the works. Sugarman's had his blinds down for the past fortnight and there's always a new person with a briefcase going in there. I'd try and ask his PA, but he's been chopping and changing them on a daily basis.'

'I don't know,' John started, waiting for Ron to fill his water bottle. 'I want to say the blame should be placed on the rhetoric currently coming out of educational jargon HQ. About how you should be able to walk into a classroom and not be able to tell who the teacher is, but should be immediately able to tell what the learning objective is and what stage of the lesson you're at. However, it's probably something trite like the fact she couldn't stand in her heels for ten minutes without damaging her achilles. Or that she had a deadline to submit and file all the observations for Sugarman and realised it was tomorrow.'

'Why shouldn't you know who the teacher is?' Ron inquired, running through his warm-up routine, which he assured himself was producing results.

'I'm not sure. Allegedly the children should be the leaders of their own learning and the driving force of where that takes them, but as far as I'm aware, that would mean half of them (in the UK at least) not bothering to do maths. It was probably a statement intended to refer to the fact we don't want children rote learning by having someone constantly standing at the front and dictating the lesson, but the education minister has taken it literally and made certain it's been passed down without any deviation. It leaves those doing the educating nervous to stand and explain a task, as though pupils are going to figure out equivalent fractions via telepathy.'

'So what do you think she's going to say?' Ron asked, adjusting the peak of his cap as though the light shining from behind John was blinding and not a fifteen watt bulb.

'I've no idea. To be honest I just need to smile and nod. Only three weeks until the holidays, then seven more and its summer and then there's only three-hundred and sixty-five days until the contract's over.'

'What a way to be thinking.'

'I'm not the only one. Fergie has a countdown timer on her phone and I've walked past countless laptops with a tab open on job websites. If all else fails, I'll do a Carl.'

'I wish I'd been there to witness it,' Ron said, going through some final limbering.

'It's up there with the Pistols playing Lesser Free Trade Hall,' John remarked, wishing he could return to the event. 'The amount of people giving you "first hand" accounts must be ten times as many as were in attendance. Although I'm sure some are there to record your reaction.'

'It wouldn't surprise me,' Ron admitted. 'It wouldn't surprise me at all.'

33.

It was precisely a week later that John was informed his feedback had been typed up and was ready. During that time Welk, Pond and Shaft had returned to their hermetic existence. Gunt could be seen at all times of the day wandering to and fro, stopping for a chat, sitting with a coffee, phone in hand and seemingly uninvolved in the whole educational process. He had asked John a couple of questions in the corridor and John had answered them frankly, though not completely frankly, and Gunt had nodded like those were the exact answers he had expected and tottered off to continue his eternal lunch hour.

In her office, it was Welk alone who had given him his feedback, which came in the form of a single target. She pushed the sheet across her desk dismissively.

A poor standard of Learning Environment. Requires immediate improvement.

John raised his eyebrows quizzically, clicking the pen that had been left by the chair's previous occupant. Welk had already placed her signature in the bottom right hand corner. She opened her black book and read the sentence typed onto the paper. She read it a second time and still John's expression hadn't altered.

'Are you referring to my booth?'

'The physical environment of what encompasses one's learning space produces a profound impact upon the psychological effects of a child's learning. In what ways does it showcase a Kindness and Life Long Learning Love?'

John had reminded himself as he'd made his way up to the office, that he would smile and nod at all that was said. He would exit as soon as possible and then distribute the paper into the bin beside his desk and return to lesson planning. Yet despite his head moving back and forth, he couldn't help but respond.

'None of my children see my environment though. They don't know what I look like unless they're on the field during the extra sport hour. I bet they wouldn't be able to locate my workspace on a plan.'

'Your learning environment,' Welk corrected him. 'What does it say about you as a teacher? What work have you displayed that you and the children are proud of? What have you created and crafted as a class to bring about unity and a sense of identity? What do you think your classroom currently tells me about you and your understanding of Kindness and Life Long Learning Love, Mr Downton?' Welk asked, her head tilted to the side, mimicking the movement of Sugarman's.

'So despite the two emails regarding the photocopying budget needing to be curtailed, one of which I think I received yesterday, you want me to print a lot of coloured sheets out to stick up in my booth, to show you the work I'm doing and inspire my children through extrasensory perception?'

'I'm quite certain I said nothing of the sort,' Welk responded. 'I understand that for those who lack the experience and expertise of those in ASLTT, these feedback sheets can seem daunting, overwhelming and difficult to understand. But they are produced to help and I am here to assist in making you a better Primary Educational Instructor for the children that are privileged to be part of our wonderful establishment.'

'So could you clarify exactly what you're looking for? The extent of the decoration perhaps, in order to assist me,' John asked.

'What I will do is go on another learning walk in two weeks' time and make another assessment from the feedback I have given you.'

'One of the walls? A couple of print outs? Some photocopies of our longer writing tasks? Should I concern myself with some border roll?'

To this Welk nodded.

'We will use the boxes on the sheet to showcase whether attainment has been achieved or if it remains an issue. I will give some group feedback in our meeting this afternoon as to the overall perceptions ASLTT have of the primary department and the educators that help to supplement its productivity. Oh, and Mr Downton, don't forget your paper. I wouldn't want any reason for your target, an integral piece of data that will inform your appraisal cycle, which will inform your bonus, to bypass you.'

As those in the department walked in for the first official meeting post Carl, they were met not by security guards and CCTV cameras as had been rumoured, but by the presence of Mr Sugarman and Ms Gillies sitting centrally against the far wall. Welk, Shaft, Pond, Gunt, Brewer, Craft and Latte were fanned out either side of them in diminishing importance. They came across as an ornate chess set with Craft and Latte squashed in the corners, like a pair of pillars guarding the gates.

Sugarman stroked his tie, watching each person who entered until they had found themselves a vacant camp stool. Now and again he would turn and whisper, usually to Gillies, though Welk too received information. The women's reactions were identical. Brief nods and stern expressions never faltered. Pond and Shaft might have been given bishop and substitute knight rankings respectively, but judging by the way they stared, refusing to cast a conciliatory glance along their line, they could have been Victorian children recently reprimanded for failing to observe the *speaking only when spoken to* rule.

'Ominous,' Jenny whispered, taking a seat beside John in the middle row, her laptop poking out of her bag. Strands of her hair were loose from her ponytail. She checked past John at the local hires, grouped together, silent and conspiring. They were lip reading each other and ready for another spectacle. John wondered how matters were dealt with in the local schools they had grown up in? How their perception of a western culture had been warped by their exposure to this organisation. What did they go and tell their friends? The same as he told his own?

Sugarman rose, gaining leverage from the two arm rests. He appeared to have grown since John last saw him, expanding like some dying star. His tie covered his fly. A dog's tongue wagging from beneath his waistcoat.

'We're here to talk about next year.' He paused as if he expected a barrage of voices haranguing every word, but like all those meetings that had come prior to Carl's show, the room remained passively engaged. 'There are going to be some changes and though we are still in discussion regarding the fine print, rather than burden you with all of them at once, we have decided to deliver them in segments.' Another pause. Another silence. 'Having concluded our own research we realised that the educational day requires extending and so from next year it will continue to 1630 with our extended activity programme running until 1730. Though there will also be a spectacular opportunity for all staff to benefit beyond that as we look to deliver a boarding style environment in order to fully develop the whole child.'

'Does this mean we're going to be given new contracts?' Jenny whispered, fiddling with her protruding laptop.

'Was there a question?'

Jenny sat back properly in her seat, checked either side and then up at Sugarman.

'Just making sure my laptop was secure,' she claimed, her posture more rigid than before. Sugarman's stare was still upon her, though she didn't wilt, rather her pleasant smile evoked memories of the previous meeting for those on her side of the board.

'In order to ensure that all ten lessons will be an equal length of a shortened fifty-five minutes,' Sugarman began, 'we will be reducing the lunch period by half an hour. There will also be one extra period given over to a specialist drama tutor. In order for everyone to have a clear picture of the gains for both students and staff, I have printed out timetables for you to view. Now I am hoping to receive some questions whilst these are handed out. Yes?'

'Sorry, I'm not sure if my calculations are correct, but from all you've said, what with the extended length of the day and the lunch break halved, ten lessons will be an hour each and yet you said they will be fifty-five,' one of the Earlier Years Developing into Primary Phase Teachers said. His question was met by nodding from Sugarman.

'Yes, the fifty-five minutes allows for a five minute theoretical hand over when children would be leaving the room and going to a specialist, or in the case of Post-Primary, making their way to their next lesson.'

'But since the majority of our lessons are back to back…'

'All lessons will be fifty-five minutes,' Sugarman said, as sheets of paper were distributed by Kate via the local hire.

'So this means the whole faculty, from Pre-Primary Early Year Developers through to Sixth Form will be running on the same timetable?' Jenny asked, as unbeknownst to most of the room, Kate began collecting in the sheets no sooner than she had distributed them.

'That is correct,' Sugarman replied, sensing a distraction was required noting the anguish on Kate's face and the whispering spreading from the local hire. 'Do you have a problem with that?'

'Well I just thought that there are probably a few discrepancies in the learning habits and daily lifestyle of children from three years old to sixteen. I mean would you expect them to go to bed at the same time?'

Guarding the papers close to her chest, squeezing them in the hope they might disintegrate, Kate crept around the edge of the room heading for the exit.

'Do you know what the problem is with this section of our educational facility? Expectations are rock bottom,' Sugarman growled, pointing an accusatory finger not just in Jenny's direction. 'There's always a question of "are the children doing too much?" "Are the children being given enough playtime?" Play time is not learning time. These are the leaders of the future. They will lead not dread. If we're going to succeed as an establishment we need to have the highest expectations across the whole facility. What happens in primary and pre-primary effects work rate further up the learning ladder,' he added, the rising volume of his tirade doing little to mute the growing fervour of mutterings relating to the papers Kate had handed out.

'I'm sorry, is there a more important matter we should be dealing with?' he suddenly asked, as the message filtered its way down from the local staff to Jenny, who whether she liked it or not, had been ordained with the role of spokesperson. John couldn't remember if she had been a union representative at home or if she just had the look of one.

Aghast, she shook her head, checking down to the original source to clarify all she was hearing was true.

'Those papers were this meeting's minutes!'

There was no real level of shock.

'Preposterous.'

'It said we had come to a unanimous agreement on extending the day,' Jenny replied, still receiving details.

'Those were classified documents that required shredding. Miss Kate had realised her mistake and that is why she recalled them,' Sugarman answered, close to yelling. 'And,' he continued, making it clear that Jenny was going to have no further statement in the matter. 'Even if they were this meeting's minutes, which would showcase an immense efficiency on behalf of ASLTT, there is no debate on the length of the school day. It is being expanded and if you do not wish to play a part in that, then by all means you are free to leave our fine establishment whenever you like.' He turned, his shoulders raised like some ravenous bear. 'You and you,' he bellowed, pointing at Pond and Shaft, who scurried after him as he exited.

In the vacuum, staff on both sides of the divide stared at their feet and cast sheepish glances, like they were part of some awkward pre-teenage dance. Eventually, Margaret Gillies found her voice,

'Well, that concludes today's meeting. I'm sure we'll have the minutes with you shortly.'

John followed her into the corridor.

'Mrs Gillies. Margaret. Hi,' he said, the voices of dissent filtering out in the other direction. 'I was just wondering if I could speak to you about my football manifesto. Have you managed to read it?'

'Oh yes,' Margaret replied. 'I read it straight after you sent it to me. It's a very comprehensive document indeed. There's lots of knowledge and some sensible ideas compiled within it.

'Thank you very much,' John said, envisioning the next steps to be taken, addressing the players, laying the foundations of a dynasty. 'So how do we go about its implimentation then?' he asked, a budget request saved in his draft folder.

'It's very dark down here don't you think? Not to worry though, the lighting system is nearly complete and ready to be rolled out. If it had already been we would be bathed in light right now.'

'That's great. It's a wonderful feeling when a plan comes to fruition, like with the football.'

'It's going nowhere.'

'Nowhere? Sorry, I thought you just said it was full of sensible ideas?'

'Oh, there's no doubt about that, but unfortunately I'm no longer in a position to make decisions regarding recreational, or out of class based, activities,' Gillies started, folding her arms as she broke eye contact.

'But you said you would pass it on. Surely I, you, we, can talk to the relevant person?'

'As far as I'm aware, there is no relevant person. Certainly there's no position regarding football or footballing activities. We do have a new position opening, but in terms of sports we will be pushing forward with in our programmes of study next year, football will not be one of them. Now you'll have to excuse me, because as the new Head of Liaising with Services in the Sectors Between A-E, I have another meeting I must attend.'

34

Catrina was coated in bubbles. John watched her from behind a pane of glass, her head on a pillow filled with herbs. He rested on his side, head propped by his right hand, bath robe sagging open loosely, ankles crossed. The TV was on mute, running headlines from BBC World News. The same six stories had been on repeat for the past three hours.

'Do you think it exemplifies the international system or it's an anomaly?'

Catrina raised an arm and blew the bubbles. They scattered in clumps, a couple sticking to the glass. She attempted to draw a face in them with a finger but they morphed into an oily residue. 'I mean should I look for something else abroad or go back home?' With her feet, Catrina turned the dial to drain the bath.

'They always told me to join a union at home but I never did. I'd join three out here if I could. I used to assume local educational authorities were a bane, a nagging shopkeeper. But where are they to come in and draw up an agenda to bring us out of special measures? To explain to those at the summit of the hierarchy that their positions shouldn't provide impunity? And who is this governing body that allegedly makes rounds once a month telling us we're constantly improving despite the objective evidence to the contrary? I'm assuming they insinuate we're ever more successful because all they look at is the box marked total and more money equates to a larger student intake. But a school isn't a company. The rhetoric should be Marxist not capitalist. We should be about reaching people, not reaching into their pockets. Who's policing our school and others of its ilk? We're like those Victorian alchemists and their potions promising weird and wonderful cures. It's utter bollocks. Laissez faire. It's no wonder the French Revolution took place. You know I've always wondered why the Europeans and South American nations simply didn't cede from FIFA, but they don't know anything else. You start making excuses for the establishment and they make you accessories. There are people who've been here for four or five years, have signed two extensions and yet hate it with as much fervour as I do. Do they think they deserve it? Is it somehow deemed safe because it's all that they've come to know? It's like Sugarman's speech about expectations, what does it say about the capabilities of the Sixth form students about to go off to university that they're on an equal timetable with four year olds?'

The drain gurgled.

'And don't start a meeting with the term "discussion" if you've already made a decision. They're simply attempting to elicit a response that runs somewhere close to their actions so everyone believes they've had a say in their future. What did Sarah Conner say in *Terminator 2* about "no fate"? She'd clearly never worked for whatever it is we're currently known as. Honestly, if anything else happens, I'm doing a Carl. This camel is loaded with straw. When I was home I used to have the odd complaint, who doesn't. You can't live in your own utopia in another person's establishment, but it certainly didn't occupy me like this, bait me, rile me, have me incessantly questioning every decision that's made. You know what it's like?' John continued, as Catrina perched on the lip of the bath facing him, skin radiating a warm pink glow.

'An absent father. There's no love or care or compassion. Promises are broken consistently and in an attempt to please us, the children, it's money. As if it's not a job but an extra reward for following the rules. Pocket money. I've lost count of how many times I've heard the word "bonus" as either a threat or alleged incentive. It's in our contracts, it's not as if it was suddenly proposed halfway through the year like the extra duties or additional hours to next year's weeks. And if it's not money or the importance of money that's being touted as a reason, then it's a fabricated job title. All of a sudden someone's walking with a spring in their step for a couple of days because they've had assistant or deputy or head or leader, or in this place all four, prefixed to a new moniker. Until they realise that not only are the same people who were above them still residing at an elevated level in the hierarchy, but someone else has randomly been added to strengthen the tree's roots. The flow chart here is more convoluted than at a Russian accountancy firm.'

Catrina leaned forward and tapped the glass with a nail, drawing John's attention to the fact her legs were spread wide.

'Are you done?' she asked, her skin raised with gooseflesh; tender and hairless. There was a light bruising on her knees. 'Is there anything else I can do to make you stay?' she asked, sucking her fingers one after another.

John let the robe fall to the floor. He wanted her. Hands around her neck. Breasts pressed tight against the glass. But as he reached the bathroom door he discovered it was locked. Catrina giggled, blowing him a kiss as he returned before her, the condensation of his breath visible. She spread her labia, revealing the pink flesh. That was how she would look if he could turn her inside out. She circled the hole with the tip of her index, bringing it back to her tongue.

'Tastes like someone's already been there,' she whispered, hand pushed against the glass, hidden by John's own. 'Do you want to watch a magic trick?' she added. 'One, two, three.' And in the blink of an eye they disappeared.

35.

The alarm reminder on John's screen buzzed, the message arriving with an explanation in detailed steps of what he was expected to do next. He exited his booth, sauntered to the end of the aisle and proceeded to do a couple of star jumps, staring up at the dot of red light, counting down slowly from ten as he did. Reaching zero he gave one final wave and headed back to continue his geography class. On the brink of entering his booth, his replacement made her way past. A post-primary science teacher. One who had allowed her alarm to ring for longer than necessary (either that or she had clicked on the tab to read the guidelines in full). She did nothing to acknowledge him as she broke into a jog.

Five times a day. John's next foray to the sensor was due ten minutes into the final period. Prior to that was an appraisal meeting regarding next year that he had been forewarned about only yesterday. He had gone to query whether it was an appraisal meeting for this year or an agenda meeting for next, but since the full installation of the new lighting system, all members of ASLTT had been unavailable. It transpired that those who fitted the system had placed in a solitary motion sensor for the whole building at the far end of the Educational Curriculum Transfer Hall. An extremely sensitive one.

Since everyone was hidden away in their booths and it required vigorous movement to work, a rota had been drawn up amongst those ground floor staff. Someone had suggested one of the large blow up men filled with air that waved and shook outside of second hand garages, but they had been dismissed on health and safety grounds. At present half the booths had been supplied with desk lamps and an email had gone round citing the delight at the organisation being at the forefront of promoting global conservation energy concerns and enabling staff exercise and alertness breaks to combat DVT and carpal tunnel syndrome.

At his previous slot John had watched all eight of the Local Maintenance and Support Service staff milling underneath the sensor wearing their empty tool belts. They were armed with their Lyonton issued hammers pointing up at the blinking light with various whacking actions.

Mr Dowtn wen duz this work bein bye

At the beginning of his tender John would have corrected the sentence, now he simply typed 15.

15 hors

No, secs.

Sex

Secs is short for seconds. You have fifteen minutes, he scribed as quickly as possible.

He leaned back in his chair, conscious of how loud his typing had sounded in this new vacuum of silence. People, himself included, now sat at their desks peeking out through the cracks awaiting the next blackout as though it would bring more than just a slate of darkness.

K

His interview, for whatever it might transpire to be, was taking place in the Grainger Suite with someone he had never heard of, but titled themselves a board trustee.

According to the map that had been attached to the meeting request, the Grainger Suite was the old example pod and before that the ICT room, which was no longer beside the stationary and stock room, but rather the Longbottom Quarters.

John assumed they had always been titled with such grand names after Lyonton alumni, but had adopted the moniker of whatever purpose they were serving at the time. The corridor had even been labelled The Delacour Gallery.

Since he had received the message, John had been mentally drawing up a list of bullet points, preparing answers to questions and rephrasing his own sentences to make points in a subtler manner. He had reached the stage where the amount of points had grown longer than his capacity to recall them and with the appointment scheduled for thirty minutes, there was no way he had time to discuss and bring them to light in a sensible fashion. He had, therefore, condensed his issues down to five main topics he was determined to receive full clarification on.

At lunch he was on duty with Fergie, who was already striding purposefully down their allocated aisles of inspection. He slowed his pace once he caught up with her, shoulder to bicep.

'How's it going?'

She rolled her eyes.

'It's getting to the point where even shopping can't bring a smile to my face.'

John nodded, squeezing her, waiting for her to divulge.

'So two days ago, Pond dropped by to inquire which year group I would like to teach next year. I said Pre-Primary. Actually I didn't, I said Early Years, exactly like I did in my initial interview. She sort of winces, half smiles and then asks me if the equivalent of Year 4 will do as that's where Welk has placed me. She then asks if there's an assistant I have in mind who I would enjoy collaborating with. I just stared at her until she left my booth.'

'Equivalent of Year 4?'

Fergie shrugged, her arms folded across her chest.

'There's something stranger than usual afoot in our gloriously opaque establishment. Did you receive an email about a meeting for next year?' she asked, skirting round the Head of Number, Shape and Measure in the Upper Post-Primary Phase, who had taken it upon himself during lunch to dress in Lycra and perform a thousand burpees in front of the sensor.

'Yeah, mine's at the end of next period,' John replied, checking his phone to see if there were any further updates regarding his appointment.

'And you noticed how they'd titled all the rooms and corridors after *Harry Potter* characters?'

'Oh yeah,' John remarked, as a dawn of realisation swept upon him. 'I can't say that I paid the books or films that much attention,' he added, leading Fergie to tut and describe who each of the characters mentioned in the plan were, though this did little in the way of offering an explanation as to why they had been incorporated.

Unable to offer any discourse upon the books or their spin-off products, small talk drifted onto recent films they'd watched, what was presently on at the English Language cinema and the long eight-week summer holiday.

'I'm going home for the first two weeks. I've packed two suitcases so that when I leave next year I don't have too much to ship. I've promised myself I'm going to stop buying so much crap. I own eight plates, six glasses and three types of cheese grater. There is one of me. What possessed me to purchase them all?'

'The last person to enter my flat said it felt like a prison. I think I'm going to donate my entire wardrobe at the end of next year and fill my suitcase with souvenirs instead,' John said, their duty almost at an end.

'If it makes you feel any better,' Fergie said, retrieving her phone. 'Our contracts now officially have under eight thousand five hundred hours remaining.'

'And as they say, time flies when you're having fun.'

36.

An internet search did nothing to unveil any hints or clues as to the reason for the character names or who the trustees of the school now were. According to the educational facility's website, they were still Lyonton school.

Within the glass walls of the Grainger Suite sat a professor, his beard styled to a long, grey point. The middle of his head was bereft of hair, giving the appearance of an immaculately groomed Dickens. He had surrounded himself with leather bound books, a couple of potted herbal plants, a quill, a stack of empty test tubes where a Newton's Cradle should have been and despite the fact the air-conditioners were out of service, he was wearing what looked like a Celtic scarf. There wasn't a piece of electronic equipment in sight. Behind him, hanging in a frame (that judging by the corner joists had been knocked up by members of Maintenance and Manual Support Services) was a giant plan of the school grounds.

John knocked on the tempered glass and was beckoned in by a grandiose sweeping of the arm.

'Mr Downton.'

John nodded, accepting the offer of the chair; somewhere in the city an English themed pub was missing a piece of furniture.

'I'm glad you could join me so as to discuss your prospects for the forthcoming year.'

The room smelt like a forest, there were sprigs of bracken by his feet.

'I'm sorry, I probably failed to read the email properly, but would you mind explaining to me who you are before we start?' John asked, noticing the scarf did not bear the emblem of any football team.

'Certainly, I'm Professor Dimbledore. I was appointed to the board of Trustees by Mr Sugarman when the establishment cut ties with Lyonton, England. I am Head of Proposed Services and Structures and am here,' he ended, building to his conclusion by raising both arms, 'to work my magic for everyone involved in this institution.'

'Right.'

'What we are undergoing here is an overhaul in the image of our brand,' Dimbledore enthused. 'And we want you to be a part of that. Now looking at you sitting here, I'm thinking this is the type of man who likes to video the action, doesn't care that there's a husband in the picture: ruthless, merciless. You know what sort of people display these traits?'

'Psychopaths? Bankers? Lawyers?'

Dimbledore laughed heartily, his chin squeezing into his neck to create a noise meant for a body far larger than his own.

'I should have added quick-witted too. They're all good answers, but of course the answer is, Slytherin.'

'Of course.'

'You see from all the research that has been conducted, we found Hogwarts is now the most famous and beloved school throughout the world. One which every child would dream of going to and being educated at. The name is associated with greatness, with achieving beyond what we think to be physically possible, yes?'

'This is why there's no need for my football programme next year, you're going to have them playing Quidditich instead.'

'Precisely! Out with the Old World and in with the new. We've been so innovative here in the past: complete virtual learning, energy efficient lighting, community ground sharing. This will go beyond that. It's like moving straight from chalk and slate to Ipads. Can you imagine that? Sitting there in your Victorian classroom scribing away in chalk when all of a sudden someone walks in with a touch-screen? Your mind would explode. You would be convinced it was,' arms raised aloft again, 'magic!'

'So our curriculum is going to revolve around online alchemy?'

'Not online, no. Hogwarts is a boarding school and so the current residential properties for staff will be undergoing a makeover to prepare them for our first batch of witches and wizards,' Dimbledore exalted, his enthusiasm showing no signs of waning.

'Sorry, there's a lot to take in. Can I just clarify so far? Number one, we're going to be called Hogwarts International School. Number two, teaching of magic and other fictional material will be included in a revised curriculum. Number three, I'll be living in some new location Hogwarts have demarcated for staff,' John said, thinking that "spells" might be a good topic for his forthcoming Poetry unit. It would provide a good cross-curricular link with art too.

'Yes, yes and no,' Dimbledore answered. 'Moving is entirely down to you. What I mean to say is there will be an accommodation allowance and there are plenty of boxes on site that could be used for packaging, but the physical removal of your goods to wherever you choose is down to you.'

'Right, okay, so let us delve a little more into point two. I assume you're not setting up recruitment stalls at every WICCA event.'

Dimbledore asked him to pause as he wrote this down, placing not just stars at the corners of the word, but wizard's hats and brooms too.

'So what do you expect from staff? To retrain? To spend the summer gathered round cauldrons?'

'Hold it again! Great publicity shot,' Dimbledore interjected, flipping the page of his un-ruled, leather bound book. 'I suppose,' he continued, 'that it's all a bit cloak and dagger, hocus-pocus if you will. Just like that photo opportunity of us all stood around a bubbling cauldron, it's the image that counts. We need to have children and parents believing they are partaking in daily magic. That they are growing stronger as sorcerers and their cohort of friends are on a scholarly journey to defeat evil and finish their studies here triumphant.

'Perception is everything. You've heard of Troy, we all have. The story from *The Iliad*. The Trojan Horse. The allegory for never trusting your enemy, of being wary as to whom you accept into your society. Scholars have argued for millennia whether it was fictional or not, and if it *were* real, where exactly the famous city once stood. There is some evidence in the Turkish province of Canakkle that suggests the city was there, but this does nothing to clarify the site in the minds of the people. It is only once Hollywood donated the horse it built for the film that tourists started coming in their droves and acknowledging that now it must be real.'

'So you want me in a pointy hat eccentrically waving a wand around for a year?' John asked, his goal of acquiring a headship in five years' time turning to dust.

'Not just that, we want you to dye your hair blonde, slick it back and become Mr Malfoy!' Dimbledore exclaimed, rising to his feet as if wishing to dub John with the title immediately.

'Wasn't he a pupil?' John asked, foreseeing the documentary. Imagining the school going viral for a few days. People back home wondering if it was a spoof, chuckling at interviews with Dimbledore announcing they were truly a school of witchcraft and wizardry.

'No, Head of Slytherin. It is the logical step for Draco according to the fans. A tamer, a slightly lighter house, but one that still has an edge. Bad Boys who still remember their P's and Q's in the right circumstances.'

'Head of House? That sounds like a rather large promotion?'

'Why of course!' Dimbledore proclaimed, producing papers from a drawer. 'The whole school will be awarded a promotion.'

'Right, so Welk, Pond, Shaft, Gunt, Brewer will all be raised into higher roles too?'

'Exactly! The current hierarchy of the establishment will remain in place for the forthcoming transition. All of the members of ASLTT you've mentioned have already signed on and all you have to do to join them is sign here, here and here and,' he flicked to the fourth page, 'date here.'

John accepted the quill and stroked the edges of the feather, smoothing the fibres together as one, then handed it back and thanked Dimbledore for his time.

'You err, haven't signed anything,' Dimbledore noted, dipping the nib in the ink again. 'Did I mention it comes with an extra two thousand per annum. Head of Slytherin. Mr Malfoy. Mr Downton.'

37.

With six weeks of the school year remaining, there still hadn't been a whole school official statement on all the changes that were to be implemented and how the school was to run come August. This didn't mean that the climate of change couldn't be noticed. There had been an eighty percent increase in black. Meetings were now referred to as covens. Paper was obsolete in the stationary room as scrolls were handed out (most of which the local hire had dyed with coffee granules and burnt at the edges). All the desks now held space for a quill and ink. The IT department was now known as W.I.T.C.H and local hire wore scarves highlighting their preferred choice of house.

John and Ron made their way to the sport's hall with the understanding that the previous game of badminton might have been their last as equipment deemed unnecessary was sold off.

'It took less than three days for me to fill the dorm rooms,' Ron said, as they yanked open the storage cupboard to find a set of posts still stationed in the far corner. 'Calls, emails, faxes, walk-ins — I was receiving one hundred and twenty per day.'

'But you still don't know how it's going to run?' John asked, unravelling the net.

'All I know is what the rooms will look like. People signed then started asking questions and I told them they'd have to wait for the brochure, which I was supposed to have received last week. Sugarman told me Gillies was sorting it out, so...'

Out of the thirty-three new staff who had arrived in August, Ron was one of four who had re-signed. Unlike the other three he was pragmatic about the whole ordeal. He had been offered a bonus for filling each boarding house and another bonus for every extra fifty students than the six hundred and twenty already enrolled.

'It's going to pay for a deposit on a four bedroom house,' he'd said. 'Plus I'm out of the loop on the "education" side.'

As for the others who'd signed on for the new franchise, they could be found in the lunch hall or corridors announcing how it was going to be "different, completely different" particularly between themselves.

Fergie's meeting with Dimbledore had been briefer than John's. By the time she went, word had spread. The Head of Proposed Services and Structures had offered her the role of Ginnie Weasley (a role she had dressed for to attend conventions at home), but when he'd responded to her question of whether she could see the job specifications by proclaiming that Mrs Welk was in the process of sorting them, she had wished him all the best.

'Did you hear what happened to Serge?' John asked, flicking a practice serve high for Ron to smash.

'Hasn't he moved to Tehran?'

'They told him he would have to learn all the rules for Quidditch, and that as they suspected they wouldn't have all the equipment for the start of the year, he would be using janitor's mops, brushes and possibly dustpans. When he told them he didn't think it sounded plausible, they said with that attitude he could go. Alas, the school in Iran where he was supposed to start in August were keen for him to arrive early, so he flew the next day.

'They told the children in his classes that at this stage of the year they were now experts and that each of them would be teaching their favourite sport to the rest of the class. From what I've heard, football lessons compromise of playing the latest FIFA and since there's no one around to do final practical assessments, this is how they're being judged. Leadership are heralding it as revolutionary break-down of barriers, levelling the playing field in terms of gender and ability. Maybe there's hope for you in badminton yet.'

Their post-game routine now included at least one drink in a newly opened bar down one of the alleys behind the accommodation buildings. It was out on the street, literally, a pop-up stall taking up a portion of the pavement now the weather had improved and was edging into the mid-thirties as it had been when they first arrived. They walked at a stroll, promenading almost.

'So, I know where I'm going to be come August, but what about you?'

John shrugged as he swigged from his water bottle.

'I don't know. I've had one interview for Moscow, one for Riyadh and I've two for home this weekend, so I'm hoping to know by Wednesday. I think I'll ship everything home except for a week's worth of clothes and travel west for a few weeks by bus and train, see how far I can go. What do you plan to do with your miserly seven weeks?' he asked, jumping up onto the curb to avoid a stream of mopeds.

'Remember I told you I'd been in Mongolia for a week before I came here? Well I hired a car and all I listened to was the BBC World Service. I'd forgotten it existed. I thought it had been made obsolete by the internet and digital radio and gone the same way as phonographs, but the stereo auto-tuned in the middle of the pips; the same ones my dad would listen to poolside when we ventured to Spain or Greece for our winter holiday over New Year. From what I can recall it sounded the same, like listening to dinosaurs or our ancestors regaling only the facts and stories of the utmost importance.

'So there I was on my way to the giant statue of Chinggis, when on comes this story about Cambodia and the genocide trials. It was a Scottish guy being interviewed, one whose brother had been in the country at the time the Khmer Rouge took over. I can't recall what he'd been doing there, but he, along with any other foreigners who had been "trespassing" on Cambodian land, was rounded up and tortured into a false confession that he was working for the CIA. It's always the CIA isn't it?

'The brother read sections of the confession and explained how his brother had mixed in coded messages to their mum, knowing the document would be kept. Then he tells the interviewer about how throughout the trial Comrade Duch is sitting, unflinching. The man meeting his stare when required, wiry, like some gentle martial art's teacher, hands resting on his knees, listening as though to an audio book with no twists in the plot.

'The interviewer asked how he thought his brother had died and it must have been a question he's contemplated every day for the past thirty years, because his voice doesn't crack. You can't hear the tears. He says that he hopes he went swiftly, that the guards took their aggression too far and bludgeoned him to death, because if not it meant he was buried and burnt alive.'

The designated space of their bar was marked by a lighter coat of cement that had been poured and left to set as it lay, a work site accident. At one side there was a man at a barbeque with skewers of assorted meat he pulled from an ice box. Five metres away, as if they were competing stalls rather than a single enterprise, a woman milled between half a dozen larger cooler boxes filled with refreshments.

John and Ron had on occasion stayed until the embers of the coals were the only light and had been forced to use the screens of their phones to navigate their way home. But usually, come seven to half past, the stock had run dry and there was pressure to vacate the collapsible camping chairs whilst the sun was still up. They each took a beer from one of the cooler boxes and sat in collapsible camping chairs.

Ron lowered his beer to the floor, the bottle leaning towards his chair on the uneven ribs of the concrete. Thich Qua'ng Duc dissolving into a grotesque screaming waxwork – human beings burnt surprisingly quickly.

A man struggled past on a bike with both tyres short on air. A couple of patrons were replaced as they left their seats. The barbeque sizzled and the conversation amongst the locals scratched around them like alley cats. Across the road a man wearing the remnants of flip-flops hawked three times and spat the deposits in the gutter. John finally spoke, brought out of his trance by the perspiring bottle sending a trickle down his arm.

Ron lifted the brim of his cap as John started, scratching his crown before lowering the peak as a pitcher would. It wasn't official Yankees' merchandise even though the NYC was interlinked. Were those three letters copyrighted? How much did the city actually make or fail to make from the acronym, the brand, the idea of New York? It was the same with all the clothing and accessories emblazoned with the Union Jack. The belief in a perpetual Cool Britannia: The Beatles, Big Ben, The Premier League. What better advertising for London Town than the young and chic evoking an idealised version of the city by parading around their respective villages wearing the flag on their fanciest threads and most treasured bags.

'Now you've straightened your thinking cap, what would you think if you told a girl that you were leaving and she responded by asking if you would "recommend her"?'

'Is this one of those new dating apps? You know everyone always says that they've gone too far and taken the mystery out of love, but I guess it's not always love you're looking for. Or was she from an escort service? I mean I suppose I respect your opinion. It's probably a lot more valid than most people's when it comes to women. You sure it wasn't rhetorical though? She didn't swing wildly at you straight after?'

'I had to ask her to repeat it.'

Ron signalled for another beer, though the only alcohol remaining came in the form of three luminous alcopops. He indicated he would take the lot.

'And would you?'

'Absolutely. A solid five stars. I thought she might ask where I was going and say that she'd join me.'

'Instead she's keen to continue providing a service to the local community.'

'Apparently.'

'It could be worse. You heard about Trevor Shaft when he first arrived didn't you? Met a local girl, slept with her on a couple of occasions and then tried to end it. When he returned after school he discovered she'd broken in through a window and chained herself naked to the inside of the front door with the words *I'm Yours* painted in red on her stomach.'

'And?'

'She swallowed the key and told him she needed something to wash it down with. He went and called Support Services. They were too scared of harming her to use bolt cutters so they removed the door from the hinges and carried her out like Lady Godiva.'

'You think it's true?'

'Oh yeah, I've heard numerous first-hand accounts. She was screaming about being loyal and not fucking his friends.'

'I meant about Lady G?' John said, watching the woman start to stack the cooler boxes, as her husband brought the charcoal back to life with a sheet of cardboard.

Ron hummed, bending the peak of his cap as the sun became less than a sphere.

'The historian in me says it's doubtful having not been mentioned in the intervening two centuries after her death. However, for the sake of something interesting once happening in Coventry, I'm going to say yes.'

'It's funny isn't it, you come all the way out here, but you wouldn't move to Coventry. I'm certainly going to miss moments like this,' John said, ready for another drink, food on the brink of being served.

They watched the chef, his grey t-shirt just covering his paunch, which sat like some boulder, levitating, rather than drooping onto his thighs. He turned the skewers slowly, one after the other. The skinny sticks wedged so tightly the juices ran over those sandwiching them. He removed aluminium foil from a clear plastic cup and shook seasoning across the meat; Ron and John had learned to request the sticks from the edges. The woman stood counting her thick roll of faded, ripped bank notes. There wasn't an evening that had gone by, as Ron and John sat drink and kebab in hand, that they didn't ask of each other, 'is this legal?'

The length of its sustained establishment had done little to convince them of its legitimacy, though neither of the proprietors sneaked anxious glances over their shoulders and locals never gave queer or threatening looks as they passed.

Since their last visit, the duo had invested in a sandwich board they had written on in chalk, items that had sold out a faded smudge.

'They'll have menus next,' Ron said, as the skewers were placed onto paper plates.

'A veranda, flyers, available to rate on Trip Advisor,' John commented, cracking open the remaining alcopops before drying his hands on his shirt.

'Do you recall, around 2012 I think it was,' Ron began, facing out onto the road, which in the immediate vicinity was clean thanks to the diligence of the woman. 'The government changed something with the leases on high street buildings in order to try and regenerate town centres that were filled with empty lots. People were in uproar claiming that all sorts of degradation was going to pop up and yet in reality it just meant four betting shops, some café trying its luck for six months and another charity shop.'

During the brief time it had taken for John to resettle into his chair, five more punters had arrived. As well as being served drinks they were handed beer mats. Not roughly cut homemade cardboard ones, but ones that matched the premium beer that had been reserved in ice for them. It came with a complimentary bowl of peanuts.

'Next time we'll have to make a reservation.'

'Do you think it's part of their vision?' John asked, collecting three mats, flicking them and passing them over to Ron, who like an Olympic high jumper declined to come in with the bar set so low. 'When they sat down to talk about embarking on this enterprise, did they have a mission statement? Is there a three-year plan? Is there some decedent blueprint of what they wish to attain complete with a roof, waiters and a spot on Google Maps?'

'Why not a Michelin Star?'

The chef wiped his hands on his shorts and scratched the stubble at the base of his neck. Ron collected ten beer mats. He aligned them, shuffling the pack an extra few millimetres off the lip of the table and flexing his fingers from the knuckle. John balanced his beer on top of them.

'I guess I was thinking more like a chain, or a franchise.'

www.ingramcontent.com/pod-product-compliance
Lightning Source LLC
Chambersburg PA
CBHW050940050726
47592CB00007B/2370